DESIRED HEARTS

CISSY MECCA

Boldwood

First published in Great Britain in 2025 by Boldwood Books Ltd.

Copyright © Cissy Mecca, 2025

Cover Design by JD Design Ltd.

Cover Images: Shutterstock

A CIP catalogue record for this book is available from the British Library.

Paperback ISBN 978-1-83656-257-3

Large Print ISBN 978-1-83656-256-6

Hardback ISBN 978-1-83656-255-9

Ebook ISBN 978-1-83656-258-0

Kindle ISBN 978-1-83656-259-7

Audio CD ISBN 978-1-83656-250-4

MP3 CD ISBN 978-1-83656-251-1

Digital audio download ISBN 978-1-83656-254-2

This book is printed on certified sustainable paper. Boldwood Books is dedicated to putting sustainability at the heart of our business. For more information please visit https://www.boldwoodbooks.com/about-us/sustainability/

Boldwood Books Ltd, 23 Bowerdean Street, London, SW6 3TN

www.boldwoodbooks.com

For anyone learning to live a life that's fully, unapologetically their own.

THE BACHELOR PACT RULES

Never stay the night
Never date the neighbor
Never fall in love
Never say "I Do"

Fall for the dirty-talking confirmed bachelor? No way. Get stuck in a cozy, snowbound log cabin together and indulge in a scorching, no-strings fling? Maybe.

Parker Scott may have a reputation as "the nice guy," but he's also a ruggedly sexy commitment-phobe bound by a "Bachelor Pact" to never settle down. So despite the sizzling chemistry crackling between us, I don't take his flirty innuendos too seriously.

Except now we're trapped in a remote mountain paradise. One minute, Parker's a sweet-talking gentleman. The next, his whispered words in a steaming hot tub surrounded by snow and temptation threaten to make me forget why I've sworn off relationships for good.

With the weekend over, I'm hopelessly addicted to Parker's unique mix of tenderness and sin. Is this eternal bachelor perhaps not so sworn to the Pact after all? One thing is clear—with my heart once again in turmoil, I'm teetering on the edge of a decision that could rewrite the rules of my story. Again.

1

DELANEY

Cedar Falls, Finger Lakes Region, NY

Two minutes ago, I was on top of the world. Or at least, on the top of my StairMaster game. Feeling empowered. Strong. Back to my old self. Just like that, with the start of a new song, tears sprang from seemingly nowhere, unbidden. My chest tightened. Shoulders sagged. Steps slowed.

I will not cry.

Unfortunately, I knew better than that. So before embarrassing myself—the gym was packed this time of day—I jumped off and headed down to the locker room. In what felt like the only break I'd had all month, it was empty. Letting the tears flow should have felt good... A necessary release.

But nothing about this breakup felt good, certainly not the fact that one stupid song brought me immediately back to one month ago when the thought of never talking to Makis again, never having answers as to why he texted "I don't think this will work out. Would like to stay friends though" had me struggling to get out of bed three days in a row.

I had to get out before someone came in. Grabbing my coat and keys from the locker, I pulled my "Good Vibes Only" hat down further and bolted to a freezing-cold car. After a few more minutes of ugly crying, I felt enough in control to try my friend Jules. No answer.

Another press of my phone button and Pia's voice flooded the car.

"Hey there."

Her cheeriness was all it took to remind me that, despite pretending otherwise, I hadn't felt like myself in weeks. Months, actually. By the end, Makis was acting so strange, our long-distance relationship causing me so much anxiety, that my friends and family had started to notice.

That's the thing about having a "bubbly" personality and wearing your heart on your sleeve. When you weren't feeling it, everyone could tell.

"Oh, Delaney. Where are you?"

"In my car," I said.

"Driving?"

"No. Sitting in the gym parking lot."

Thankfully I didn't have to tell Pia I'd had to jump off the StairMaster and bolt out of there like someone was giving away free cupcakes in the parking lot. Which, to be honest, wouldn't be a bad way to get people to the gym. Counterproductive maybe, but...

"Did he contact you?"

"No," I clarified. "A song reminded me of him."

"Oh. Well, that will happen."

"I deleted every playlist I made when we were together. I guess it snuck through."

"There's no way to get rid of every single reminder. You guys dated for nearly eight months."

"On and off."

"Sure, but more on than off. It will take more than a few weeks to heal. Give yourself some grace."

"I'm trying," I said in earnest. "It just..." My cheeks stung. I squeezed my eyes shut, new unshed tears escaping. "This sucks so much. My heart hurts."

"I know it does. But try to remember how he made you feel these last few months. How often he made you feel poorly. You deserve someone who does just the opposite."

I took a deep, steadying breath. "I deserve to be loved, not dismissed and discarded."

"Yes," she said, knowing that was my new mantra.

"I make mistakes and have moments of weakness, but the people who are meant to be in my life love me either way, and I am worthy of their love. It's time to look forward and not backward."

"You got it. Just keep reminding yourself of that. Saying it over and over."

"This is so damn hard."

"But won't last forever. You just have to get through the tough days."

"It's feeling like wine Wednesday." I'd planned on using the night off at the pharmacy to clean my jewelry and makeup drawers, get my apartment organized. But I felt like doing that now about as much as I felt like going back into the gym to finish my workout.

"There's a couple checking in today. We're slammed at the inn. But text Jules a time and a place, she was talking about going out tonight too."

"Will do," I said, wondering for the millionth time what I would do without my friends.

"Oh, and also..."

I waited for my friend's words of wisdom.

"Makis is a giant asshole. So there's that."

I laughed. "True statement. See you later."

Hanging up, I got a look at my pale, tear-stained face. Winter sucked. Makis sucked. Men in general? Suck. Suck. Suck. I was not getting myself into this situation *ever* again. The whole "it's better to have loved and lost than never loved before" was bullshit.

I was done with love.

Forever.

2

PARKER

"There he is, the man of the hour."

As usual, Beck stood behind the bar at O'Malley's Pub, raising a hand to me as I walked through the surprisingly heavy Wednesday night crowd. Not surprising? That he was currently working a group of female tourists with his drink-making skills. His surfer good looks, slightly out of place in upstate New York, would charm every one of them. Question was, which did Beck have his eye on?

"Took you long enough," Mason said. I sat in the empty seat beside him. "The brunette," he whispered.

"Convenient of them," I said of the women, "to differentiate themselves."

One brunette. One blonde. One redhead.

"Speaking of brunettes," I said as Beck poured my beer, "where's Pia?"

Mason's fiancée was usually not far behind him, and this "celebration" was her idea.

Not that I thought a celebration was needed. I constructed a footbridge pro bono for the town because it connected a residential area with a kids' park, not for some award from the Cedar Falls Recreational Committee.

"Drinking wine with Delaney."

"Couldn't they drink wine here?" I asked as Beck pushed a beer toward me.

"Apparently not. She's going through a bad breakup."

"Who?" Beck asked. He hated not being part of a conversation.

"Nosy bastard. Go back to impressing your tourists."

"Shhh," he admonished me. "Don't want her to hear and think I'm a player."

Mason and I exchanged a glance, and we both burst into laughter. Neither of us needed to state the extremely obvious. Beck was the biggest player that either of us had ever met.

"Assholes," he muttered as a guy at the end of the bar flagged him down for a drink.

"I can't believe you haven't met her yet," Mason said, I assumed about Pia's good friend Delaney. I wasn't born and raised in Cedar Falls and therefore didn't know every single person in town like Mason and Beck.

"I don't think she's lived here full-time since you came to town," Mason said.

"But she's been here at least since Pia moved to town so she's been around since fall."

"True. But with the long-distance boyfriend, Delaney's usually out of dodge whenever she's not working."

I was about to ask him what Pia's friend did for a living when Beck reappeared.

"Round of shots for the best of us." He slid one toward each of us. As he held up his phone, a familiar face appeared.

He might be crazy as hell, but Beck was one thoughtful motherfucker too.

"Congrats on the big award," our friend Cole said through the phone. He was the only one of us not living in Cedar Falls.

"It's not a big deal," I insisted.

Cole adjusted his dark-framed glasses, which made him look every inch the college professor that he was.

"To Parker," Mason said, lifting his shot glass. "The nice one."

Even Cole lifted a shot glass. It looked like he was at a bar too, though it would be very different from this small-town Irish pub, Cole living in Manhattan and all.

"Bound by life's ride," Beck said as we all finished our familiar toast. "Here's to the journey."

Beck handed the phone to me and went back to work.

"Thanks for checking in. When you coming back to town?" I asked him as Mason looked on.

"Can't hear you guys well," Cole said.

"Never mind. We'll talk to you later."

"See ya, Cole," Mason added before Cole put up a hand, signing off.

"What's next for the big award winner?" Mason pushed his shot glass toward Beck, who grabbed it walking by. The guy was a phenomenal bartender, even if he picked up nearly as many women as he served.

"Not you too?" I took a swig of beer.

Mason almost smiled. It took a lot for the corner of his lips to actually rise. "Seriously, though. What's on tap after your weatherproofing job?"

"I was thinking we could tackle the bathrooms—"

"With you, not the inn," Mason clarified.

Since he took over his father's inn, leaving the NYPD behind and moving back to Cedar Falls last year, I moved in and helped to renovate the place. So of course Beck did too, not wanting to miss out. Thankfully, even though Mason got together with Pia, his fiancée was on good terms with us clowns and cool with the arrangement.

"Nothing major," I said. "A lot of odd jobs. Painting, tiling. We lost the apartment complex bid."

"How did Jack manage to fuck that up?"

"By being Jack."

My boss has a penchant for fucking things up.

"Park, you gotta get out on your own."

Different day, same discussion. "Yeah, yeah."

"I'm serious. You have enough jobs under your belt, and if you're staying in construction, you can't keep working for someone that flighty."

I agreed, but there were problems with going out on my own. With a college degree in business, and growing up working at my father's car dealership, I knew what it took to start my own business. It also wasn't so simple in a town this size. Jack would be madder than hell. Clients who were also friends would be forced to choose between us.

I was about peacemaking, not rocking the boat.

"The blonde just asked about you," Beck said to me, thankfully interrupting our discussion. "Said, 'Your cowboy-looking friend is hot.' Told her you weren't a cowboy, but she didn't seem to care."

"It's the boots." Mason clearly got a kick out of that description.

I was an outdoorsy guy, and did like my boots, but hiking and fishing weren't exactly the same as cattle herding.

"No, thanks," I said. "Not my type." I didn't need to look over, having already noticed the women when I came in.

Unlike Beck, I didn't make one-night stands a regular occurrence. Not that I was into relationships either. All four of us swore off on those a long time ago, although Mason apparently didn't get the memo. Or at least, lost the memo after meeting Pia.

I could hear the blonde giggling from here. Definitely not my type.

"You sure?" Beck asked, adding matchmaking to his eclectic resume.

"Positive."

"Good call," Mason said as Beck walked off. "They're barely twenty-one."

My phone buzzed. Looking at the screen, I groaned.

"What is it?"

"Shit," I said, re-reading the text. "Dad. Wants to visit this weekend."

I texted him back.

"That's... strange."

"Agreed. Something must be up. Do we have room?"

"At the inn? Sure. Valentine's Day weekend is the only one sold out in the next month. He's a real piece of work," Mason added.

A guy who cheated on my mother three times before getting caught, whose mid-life crisis started when my brothers were barely out of diapers and had never ended? "That's one word for him."

I texted back, tossed my phone on the bar, and called to Beck. "I'm gonna need another beer. Maybe a shot too."

3

DELANEY

"Jules to the rescue."

I pressed pause on the remote as Juliette, otherwise known as Jules, stepped inside waving a bottle of my favorite wine in the world.

"No," I said. "You didn't."

"Yes, I did."

Taking off her jacket, Jules put down the bottle of Aonair wine. It was a hundred-dollar bottle from a small winery in Sonoma that we only pulled out on special occasions.

And tonight was certainly no special occasion. My poor friend was in for a heap of moping and commiserating, which was why I told her to go out without me. But she refused.

"It's so cozy in here," she said, heading to the kitchen.

When I moved back to Cedar Falls, finding this old Victorian home just a few blocks off the square felt like kismet. On a quaint, tree-lined street within walking distance to the pharmacy, the only thing it needed was some fresh paint. Courtesy of my dad and his painter friend, a cheerful shade of blue greeted me every day. Before the winter hit, two rocking chairs and some hanging plants made it a perfect welcome home after a long day at work.

"You're brooding again," Jules said, handing me a glass of wine. Grabbing a fuzzy blanket, she situated herself on the other couch. "I love your house."

Jules lived in an apartment, and I'd told her more than once she was welcome to move in.

"I think you love it more than me," I said. She was staring at the stone fireplace which, unfortunately, used real wood. The aesthetic was great, but it was a pain in the ass to keep wood and get started.

"Honestly, I do. It's like a writer's paradise."

"Speaking of writing, how did that article about the birth-place of the women's rights movement do?"

Jules loved writing, but hated the fact that it was her nonfiction that brought home the bacon. "It was well received," she said, tucking her feet under her. Jules's shoulder-length black hair was held back by a bandanna. The multiple silver necklaces, always present, gave her an edgy look, exactly the opposite of my own. Red hair and a smattering of freckles tended to evoke more wholesome vibes than "girl who lives on the edge."

I took a sniff of the wine, intending to make every moment count. "I still can't believe you brought this over on a random Friday night."

Taking a sip, I let the burgundy liquid slide down my throat.

"You've had a rough week." Jules took her own sip, the sound of a crackling fire the only one to fill the room. With my TV still on pause, and the street I lived on filled with older people and almost always pretty quiet, we might as well have been in the middle of a forest. I didn't count on that as a benefit of this house, and sometimes it was too quiet for me, but at this moment, it suited us.

"The worst," I said after another few sips of wine, "is how angry I am for going back to him. I think I always knew he'd hurt me in the end. But I did it anyway."

Jules had as sordid a dating history as me and could understand. "I know," she said. "But love isn't logical. We don't always make the best decisions. But the past is in the past. Over and done with. No point in looking back. You're not going that way."

Surprisingly, I didn't feel tears forming or the tingle of my cheeks that said they were coming. My chest still hurt, but it was more like an emptiness than a knot twisting inside there. I took another sip, not wanting to put the show back on. For the past few weeks I alternated between work, the gym and home, usually numbing myself with reality TV.

All for some giant asshole who'd probably moved on the second after he broke up with me. Again.

"I'm done," I said.

"With?"

"All of it. Moping over him. Hiding in my house. Feeling like shit. I'm done."

Jules smiled. "I'd have brought the Aonair weeks ago if I knew it would be that easy."

I lifted the glass. "This helped, no doubt. But I just think... being sad only gives him more power over me. But Makis isn't in control of my life. I am. It's time to act like it."

Jules pulled the blanket over one of her feet, which were notoriously always cold.

"That's my girl."

"Remind me to listen to you next time you give me dating advice."

Jules laughed. "Which specific piece of advice are we talking about?"

"The one about not having to try so hard to make it work. If he was meant to be in my life, he would be."

"Sound advice."

"That gem is from Pia, who knows a bit about the subject."

Jules nodded. "She does. It's hard to imagine now that she and Mason had any rough patches. Clearly they were meant to be together."

"I'm happy for her," I said sincerely.

"Same. Speaking of Mason, he does have two single hot men living with him. If you really are over the asshole Makis hump—"

"First of all, no way. And second of all, no way." I took a sip of wine, wishing I could be transported back to Sonoma.

"Too soon?"

"Much. Not to mention, I dated one of them already."

"Does that really count, though? You were in middle school."

I thought of Beck when we were young and, more recently, of him slinging drinks behind the bar at O'Malley's. The vision was complete with no less than three females hanging off his arm drooling.

"Yes," I insisted. "It counts. I'm also 0 percent interested in a serial dater like him."

"You were the one who said no more relationships. I'd think he was perfect."

"No. Not perfect."

"And the other one? What's his name?"

"Parker something or other. Mason and gang met him in college."

"I've heard him mentioned here and there. Probably ran into him at some point."

"Probably," I agreed. Cedar Falls wasn't that big, and while I hadn't been back long, Jules never left. "Although you are a bit of a homebody so..."

"A bit?" She laughed.

"Okay, more than a bit."

Jules suddenly leapt up. She took my glass and headed to the kitchen. "We are opposite in so many ways," she said, refilling us.

I grabbed my phone. We'd talked about ordering some Chinese, and suddenly I was starving. "Don't they say opposites attract?" I asked as Jules came back into the living room.

"I think that's in terms of dating." She handed back my wine, now filled.

"Hmm, well, either way." I lifted my glass. As we clinked, I said, "To friends. I honestly don't know what I'd have done without you and Pia these past few weeks."

"You'd have been just fine."

"Eventually. Maybe," I said as Jules headed back to her couch. "Either way, I appreciate it. Chinese is on me. What are you getting?"

"Chicken and broccoli, white rice. And an egg roll."

You'd have been just fine.

Maybe, maybe not. Either way, I was grateful for the friendships that had helped pull me through. I'd have relapses, obviously. Memories that would undoubtedly trigger me. But the moping had to stop. He just wasn't worth it.

"It's been a while since I've seen that famous Delaney smile."

I looked up from my phone. "It's been a while since I've felt like smiling."

To think a man—no, a boy—had so thoroughly broken me. I thought I was stronger than that, but I guess life still had some lessons to share. My friends and family were all I needed. I might even put a "no boys allowed" sign on my front door.

"What's so funny?" Jules asked as I called the restaurant.

"Nothing," I said. "Just me being silly."

"Delaney. Is. Back. I love it."

"Yes," I said, waiting for an answer and hoping to convince myself it was true. "Yes, she is."

4

PARKER

"Morning, Mr. Scott."

Mason and I sat, as we did most mornings, at the kitchen island. Pia had taken her coffee to the inn portion of Heritage Hill to speak with Esther who cooked breakfast every morning for guests. The original inn was an old mansion built as a private lakeside residence in the late 1800s. The "house" side where we stayed was added on and restored twenty years ago, but under Mason and Pia's plan, all of it was getting an update. Today, though, was a day off. No work of any kind courtesy of Dad's visit.

"Always so formal," my dad said, heading to the coffee pot.

"Military guys," I said of Mason. "Also just good manners."

"Well, it makes me feel old. Parker will do just fine."

"Doesn't it get confusing?" Mason asked. "Same name and all."

Dad and I exchanged a glance. It was like looking into a mirror of the future. Though my brothers were more of a mix, I was 100 percent my father. Add a sprinkle of white hair, some wrinkles and a few extra pounds in my belly, and our similarities didn't stop at our names.

"Eh, we manage okay." My father sat down beside me.

"Good time last night," he said. We'd gone to O'Malley's, as usual. Although my father only spent about half of the night with us.

"Who was the woman you met?" I asked.

"I'm going to help Pia," my traitor of a friend said. "See you later, Mr."—Mason cleared his throat—"Parker," he amended.

Left alone with him, I tried to dredge up the same feelings I had for the guy when I was younger. When I looked up to him. Before he cheated. Before he left.

"A loan officer," he said. "Divorced and pretty good-looking too."

It had been a number of years since my parents split, but I still wasn't comfortable talking about dating with my dad. Probably never would be. Maybe if Mom dated too, it would be different. But she didn't, despite urging from my brothers and me. She said her sons and friends were enough, but I had a feeling she'd just been burned too much by Dad's infidelity to try again.

"You still up for cross-country skiing?" I asked. One thing Dad and I still had in common was anything to do with the outdoors. I had to give him credit for that, at least. He'd taught me all sorts of things, from skiing to fishing and hunting.

"Sure thing. But have to skip out on dinner."

I'd have asked why, but I already knew. My dad was so goddam predictable. Just to be sure, I said, "The woman?"

"You don't mind, do you?"

To not have to make small talk with him all day and night? "Nah," I said, meaning it. "I'm heading into town first to pick up some materials. Do you need anything?"

"Where is Lakeside Pharmacy?" he asked.

Strange question. "It's just off the square. Why?"

"Can you stop and grab a script for me?"

"For?"

"Nothing special, just forgot one of my meds. Doc called it in this morning. It should be ready by now. I thought we could stop on our way out."

Dad took a slew of medications. High cholesterol. High blood pressure. He claimed years of owning a car dealership were responsible for both, but it was more likely his affinity for bacon accounted for at least some of his problems.

"I'll grab it. Be ready in, say, an hour?"

Dad lifted up his coffee mug. "Sounds good." His smile, so familiar because it often mirrored my own, was disarming. This was probably, among other reasons, why Mom had taken him back so many times. The guy really was a charmer. It was hard to stay mad at him. "I'll be ready."

I could hear my mother's voice in my ear.

He was a shit husband, but a good father. Remember that.

It was my mom who got me speaking to him again after the third affair. My brothers had no choice since they both worked at the dealership, but Dad and I had a rocky go of it for a while there. Things still weren't back to "normal," whatever that was, but I supposed this weekend was a good thing, even if he was skipping out on part of it. Him taking two days off from the dealership was a big deal, so I'd at least make an effort.

Grabbing my jacket, I stepped out onto the thin layer of snow that had fallen last night. When I'd get back, I'd toss some rock salt on that. Mason hadn't left the inn and probably had no idea it had even snowed.

Walking up the hill, I ran to the hardware store first. Cedar Falls town center was a perfect square, its trees and gazebo now barren. In warmer weather, tourists would fill the square and blocks of shops and restaurants around it, but today there were only a handful of stragglers, mostly locals.

"Millie." I ran up to an older woman trying to open the door of a coffee shop. "Let me get that." I took her grocery bag. "Why didn't you have these delivered?"

Escorting her inside, I walked the widow to the counter.

"Walking keeps me young," she said, pulling the scarf around her neck tighter.

"Understandable, but you have to be careful. Let me bring these to your house while you get coffee," I said, already knowing she would argue with me.

"Oh, no, no," she started, but I wasn't listening.

"I'll put them by your door. Enjoy your coffee," I said as Millie chastised me until I was outside. She was a staple at The Coffee Cabin and I'd had more than one cup with her since moving here.

It was only a few blocks out of my way to Millie's house. Hers was one of my first construction jobs when I'd moved to Cedar Falls, her husband having hired us to tear down and rebuild their front porch. By the time I headed back to the square to hit the pharmacy, forgoing another coffee, my dad had texted, asking if we were leaving soon. Patience was not one of his virtues.

Opening the door of Lakeside Pharmacy, I tried to remember the last time I'd been inside. It wasn't long after I'd moved to Cedar Falls, though I couldn't remember what I'd needed a prescription for.

It was a small place with a few drug store-type items with the check-out counter and pharmacy in the back. A long, empty counter greeted me. Not completely empty, actually. A bell with a small index card with the words "ring me" scrawled on it was apparently my signal.

I rang the bell.

A woman stepped out from behind the rows of medications. I'd never seen her before.

Her red, medium-length hair was pulled back in a ponytail. She looked like an actress, though I couldn't remember the woman's name. Very little makeup and a smattering of freckles across her nose and cheeks gave her a very wholesome look.

Wholesome. And very, very pretty.

Her white lab coat gave the woman away as a pharmacist. A young one, late twenties maybe? As she approached, it was her smile that enraptured me most. That and the unusual blue-gray color of her eyes.

"Can I help you?"

Her voice was sweet. Peppy. Endearing. Like the woman herself.

"Yeah," I managed, not used to being tongue-tied. "I'm picking up a prescription for Parker Scott."

She moved to a box of bags behind her, rifling through them. "Sorry about the service," she said. "Our clerk called off, and no one was available last minute."

"You're the pharmacist?" I asked, silently kicking myself for such a dumb-ass question. Obviously she was.

"I am." She turned back around, punched something into the register and looked up as I handed her my credit card without asking the price. "Do you have any questions about this?"

Her expression was unreadable, but I was sure mine was anything but. I probably looked like a lovesick teenager or someone who'd never seen a pretty woman before.

But damn, there was something about her. It was the smile.

Lip gloss and mascara. That was all she wore, lip gloss and mascara. Why bother with anything else if you were that naturally pretty?

"No," I managed. "No questions."

It's for my dad.

Thankfully, I didn't say that out loud too. She probably already thought I had the emotional maturity of a fourteen-year-old.

"Are you from Cedar Falls?" I asked. "I don't remember seeing you around."

"I am."

My phone rang.

She handed me back my card and looked at my pocket as if to ask, "Are you going to answer that?" Why the hell wasn't my phone on silent, like usual? I wanted to ignore it. Keep talking to her. But since our transaction was over, there was no good excuse to stay, especially with my phone being really fucking annoying.

Grabbing it from my pocket, I mumbled a "thank you" and headed back out of the pharmacy.

Not surprisingly, it was my father.

"I'm in my snow pants," he said, "sweating my balls off."

Rolling my eyes, I headed out of the pharmacy and back toward the inn. "I'm on my way," I said, feeling even more like a teenage kid than I had inside the store. My father had a way of putting me on the defensive, as if I weren't a thirty-two-year-old man. "And why the hell are you wearing your snow pants?"

Thinking better of it, I added, "Never mind. I'll be there in five."

"Good," he said. "Oh, and Beck just woke up. Wanted me to ask you about grabbing a sausage and egg sandwich from The Coffee Cabin."

"Tell him I'm already running late and to eat a piece of fruit."

"He said to eat a piece of fruit," my dad told Beck, who was apparently with him still. "I won't repeat what he said."

Beck. What a piece of work.

"Fair enough. I'll be there in five."

Hanging up, I turned off my ringer and headed back down the hill, thoughts of a certain redhead floating through my mind.

Who was she?

It wouldn't take much to figure out. I'd ask Mason or Beck. Between the two of them, they knew every single person in Cedar Falls, especially the women. Hell, chances were that one of them had even dated her, judging by her age, unless she was an implant, like me.

Please, just don't let it be Beck.

5

DELANEY

Finished counting the pills, I placed them in their container along with the label, checking the information three times. It was monotonous work, and for the millionth time I wondered what had possessed me to become a pharmacist. Aside from an offhand comment from my college advisor, it had never been on my radar. Medical school? Sure. A marine biologist? For the longest time, that had been my dream. And of course, an artist would have made total sense. Instead here I was, back home, counting pills.

Stuck.

Reminding myself I was a glass-half-full, and not glass-half-empty, kind of girl, I shook off the self-pity. I'd just decided last night to stop wallowing in the post-breakup blues and wasn't going to start up with this train of thought. I'd picked my career path and had been lucky enough to land this job in a town where my parents both still lived along with old friends, and new ones too.

Count your blessings, Delaney.

The bell startled me. It was a quiet late-January day with

very little foot traffic. Not that Lakeside was a huge drug store and most people only came in for prescriptions, but we did have a few aisles of odds and ends and, in warmer months, had a steady stream of customers.

"Hey," I said, walking to the counter to find Pia there. "What's going on?"

"Surprise!" She held up a bag.

"That looks suspiciously like..." I leaned in closer. "No, you didn't?"

"Yep, I did. Mason and I went for dinner and knew you were working late." She handed me the bag. "There's a fork in there too."

"Stop," I said, peeking inside. "What do I owe you?"

"Dinner. When's your next night off?"

"Tomorrow, but—"

"Done. Let's go to The Grapevine. I'm dying for their stuffed pork chop."

"Thank you," I said, venturing a guess. "Jambalaya?"

"Obviously," Pia teased. She knew the jambalaya from a local favorite New Orleans-themed restaurant, The Big Easy, was one of my favorites. "So what was your standby?"

"A banana and bag of Ruffles."

Pia laughed. "Nice."

For some reason, packing my lunch, or in tonight's case dinner, was one of my least favorite chores. "In my defense, Becca called off. My original plan was to run out for something."

"Uh huh." Pia looked skeptical. "Oh, I forgot to tell you. That bracelet you made for me, the one with the turquoise stones?"

"Yeah?" I opened the bag. With no customers, there was no time like the present to dig in. If someone came in, I'd bring my food to the back.

"A couple checked in yesterday and she asked where I got it

from. When I told her a friend made it, she asked if you could make her one. She said, and I quote, 'whatever the cost.'"

Pia knew I only designed jewelry for friends. The idea of starting it as a business, plus long hours at the pharmacy, wasn't in my immediate plans. A girl could dream though...

"Whatever the cost, huh?" I asked, intrigued. Taking a bite of jambalaya, I groaned at how good it was. Which made me immediately think of... him. "Oh my God," I said between bites. "How about this one? The hottest guy ever came in this morning."

"Ooooh, I like it. You weren't kidding when you said you were ready to move on."

I rolled my eyes. "Trust me, I'm not going there. But you have to hear this. He was mega hot. Outdoorsy type, brown hair, very well built... even beneath a jacket I could tell."

"Sounds to me like you're going there," Pia hedged.

"I'm not, trust me. The thing is..." I took another bite, unable to help it. I was starving. Finished chewing, I said, "He was probably around thirtyish, and I'm telling you, a ten out of ten."

"Obviously there's a 'but' in there somewhere."

"A big one. He was picking up... VitalFlow."

Pia's jaw dropped. "Get out?"

"Seriously."

"Wow. That's nuts. I didn't know men could have that problem so young."

"It's much more common as men get older, but there are some things that can cause it in younger guys."

"Such as?"

"Psychological factors, medications, other health conditions. It was just... surprising."

"I bet. Tourist?"

"I assume. I've never seen him before."

"You've been MIA since coming back."

"True," I admitted. "But he definitely isn't from here. That's not a face you forget. Plus he's about our age, so I'd know him for sure."

"Did you talk to him?"

"A little." I thought back to our brief conversation. Aside from his good looks, and really affable smile, he also had one of the deepest voices of any man I'd ever met. Extremely sexy. "Poor guy."

"Seriously. That has to make it hard to date."

"Maybe he's married?"

"Was there a ring?"

"No."

Pia laughed. "So you noticed?"

"Perhaps," I admitted with another bite. "But like I said, problem or no problem, I'm not interested."

"In a relationship. But maybe a little tourist-action is just what you need to get back on the saddle."

"Thanks, but no thanks."

"So the bracelet?" Pia circled back around.

I did really enjoy making jewelry. And painting. And even pottery. My mother had been shocked I went the science route in college. She'd been convinced I would do something with art, but I had enough starving artist friends to know how viable that was as a career. When I did decide on becoming a pharmacist, both of my parents were overjoyed.

"Fine," I said. "Get her number."

"Awesome. She'll be thrilled. I also think it'll be good for you."

I knew exactly what Pia meant. Since the breakup, I hadn't picked up a paintbrush, or even entertained going into my craft studio which had been converted from the second bedroom in my house.

"Maybe," I said noncommittally. "I'm sure hanging out in a pharmacy isn't on your Saturday night to-do list. What's next?"

"I'm meeting Mason at O'Malley's. You should come. Are you done at nine?"

"Yeah. Although I don't understand why we stay open so late this time of the year. Before you, I think the last customer came in an hour and a half ago."

"Because the owner is a dipshit."

"True."

"Come on," she urged. "When was the last time you went out?"

"I go out plenty," I argued.

"Not to dinner. I mean, out out?"

"It's been a while," I admitted. "But I'm not dressed and—"

"Delaney." Pia's tone scared me.

"We'll see," I said, not willing to commit. I'd held up pretty well all day, but pretending I was okay, and totally ready to move on from Makis, had taken its toll. I also kinda wanted to go home, take a tub and then crawl into bed.

"Mmm hmm." Pia gave me the stink eye, knowing me too well. "I'm not letting you off the hook. It's time to rejoin the world of the living."

The pharmacy door opened. "Thanks for dinner," I said, moving my jambalaya to the back room. "I'll text you."

"You better," Pia warned, waving. "Talk to you later."

"Thanks again," I called, shoving dinner to the side and heading back to the counter.

"Can I help you?" I asked the stranger.

6

PARKER

"It's a big inn." I tossed Beck a beer. It was his night off, and the last thing he wanted to do was go back to O'Malley's. "We can make ourselves scarce."

As usual on a Thursday night, we were in the kitchen sitting on stools around the island.

"Scarce," Mason muttered. "As if he's ever heard the word before." He nodded to Beck.

"Hey," Beck started to defend himself.

"There are six of them, all but two are single," Mason added.

Beck closed his mouth, knowing better than to argue. If Pia was having friends over for a wine tasting—single friends— Beck would be anything but scarce.

"And it *is* a big inn," he said to me. "But we only use the house portion for ourselves, as you know."

"I do, but the reception room would be perfect for a wine-tasting night."

Part of the original structure, which was more mansion than house, the reception room had been turned into a full-blown banquet hall. Part of the renovations had been to add space to host parties and, come this summer, even small weddings, something Mason's father had always fought against. He'd wanted to preserve the quaint experience for existing guests, but just before he died suddenly of a heart attack last fall, Mr. Bennett had hired Pia to turn the inn around. Hosting events had been one way to bring in some much-needed cash.

"Not 'cozy' enough. Pia's words, not mine." Mason pulled a beer from the fridge. "So where we headed?"

"Not O'Malley's," Beck said, understandably.

"Cedarwood?" I asked.

Of all the bars in town, besides O'Malley's, Cedarwood Bar and Grill was one of my favorites. It was within walking distance, unpretentious, and typically attracted a more mature crowd.

Which is exactly the reason Beck made a face.

"You're gonna have to start dating women out of college at some point," Mason said, his voice dripping with sarcasm.

Pia swung open the kitchen double doors at that precise moment.

"Stop teasing my guy," she said, literally walking right up to Beck. For some reason, despite the fact that Pia was an intelligent, independent woman, she'd taken a liking to him. The two of them had a brother/sister relationship almost from the start. At least, after he stopped hitting on her after realizing Mason was interested.

"Thank you, Pia," he said with a wink.

"Your guy wants to stay here and drink," Mason pointed out.

"Sorry, Beck." Pia turned on "her guy" just like that. "No can do. It's strictly a girls' night."

"Who's coming?" he asked, not masking his interest in the topic.

Pia made a face but answered, "Jules, Delaney, a friend of

hers from the gym, a woman I met from the chamber of commerce—who's married—and someone she works with. Don't know her name since we haven't met."

"Is she hot?"

"The one I haven't met?" Pia asked, crossing her arms.

"No, the friend from the gym."

"I suppose. But she's also getting over a bad breakup, like Delaney."

"So it's a therapy session?" he asked.

"You are impossible. So where you guys going?"

"Cedarwood." Mason reached for Pia, pulling her next to him. "Will you miss me?"

"Oh, here we go," Beck said dramatically.

Unlike my friend, I had no problem with PDA, especially from a guy who I'd been convinced would be single forever. We all had a reason to take that bachelor pact in college, Mason included. For him, seeing his dad's heartbreak after Mason's mom died, the guy never remarrying because of it, left some scars.

We all had them.

I gave my attention to Beck. "What's in the pot now?" I asked, still thinking of our pact.

"Six-fifty, right? One hundred each to pony up and Mr. Engaged here," he said, nodding to Mason.

Pia went to the fridge and pulled out some vegetables. "I still can't believe you had to donate two hundred and fifty dollars to... that."

"A pact is a pact," Mason said, taking a swig of his beer.

"When he gets married, that'll be another two-fifty," Beck said. "The pot's growing."

Pia rolled her eyes. "I don't think I ever asked whose idea it was in the first place?" She side-eyed Mason. "Wait, maybe I don't want to know."

"It wasn't Mace," I said. "Take a guess who came up with it."

"Setting the stage," Beck said, warming up to the topic. "Someone just got dumped. We were in senior year—"

"Of college," I added.

"No shit, Sherlock." Mason put his hand around the back of Pia's neck as she cut vegetables, massaging it. This warm and fuzzy version of my ex-cop, ex-military friend would take some getting used to. "Pia knows we met Park in college."

"Anyway," Beck continued, ignoring Mason. "We were at our apartment on a late Saturday afternoon, getting ready to go out. Pregaming, you know?"

"I can only imagine," Pia said wryly.

"And that's when one of us, but not Mason, said, 'Let's make a pact right here, right now. Bachelors for life.'"

I tried not to laugh at Beck's overly dramatic storytelling voice.

"Any guesses?" I asked her.

She stopped cutting celery. "Not to be too personal," she said to me. "But I know you're not a huge fan of your dad, given everything. I'm thinking maybe that situation soured you on the whole love and marriage thing?"

"True statement," I said with a swig of beer. "But it wasn't me."

She turned to Beck. "I wouldn't have guessed you right off the bat since both your mom and dad remarried."

"Married does not mean happily married," Beck said. "Even the second time around."

Pia and Beck had grown close. No doubt she knew all about Beck's super wealthy, meddling, divorced, remarried... and did I mention controlling parents? "But I'm still guessing you. If there's anyone in this foursome who isn't into the whole relationship thing, it's you."

"Try again," Beck said, enjoying this way too much.

She looked at me, surprised. "Seriously?"

"Seriously." I shrugged. "Like Beck said, married doesn't mean happily married. I think it's almost worse that Cole's parents should have gotten divorced years ago, but didn't."

Cole's father, like our friend, was an Ivy-league college professor and lived for his job, above everything, unfortunately.

"I won't be shocked if they do separate," Beck added. "When his sister graduates high school."

"Wow. Cole. I honestly wouldn't have guessed him first. He's that anti-relationship?"

"Big time," I said as Pia began cutting celery again. "I honestly think if any of us really do stay a bachelor for life, it'll be him."

"I don't plan on settling down anytime soon," Beck said. "Some of us took the pact seriously."

"I took it seriously." As soon as the words were out of my mouth, I realized that never being in a committed relationship probably wasn't the hill I wanted to die on. It wasn't noble, or maybe even a great idea, given Mason and Pia's success story. But that was the point. All of our parents started off in love, but the only one who stayed that way was Mason's dad, who lost the love of his life way too young. "Anyway," I said, wanting to move on, "what time are your friends coming?"

"In an hour," Pia said.

"We'll finish these and get out of your hair before they do."

Beck all but pouted but finished his beer anyway. Less than twenty minutes later, ready to roll, the three of us headed out.

We were halfway up the walkway that led from Heritage Hill to the road above us which led to Cedar Falls' town square a few blocks away when a figure appeared. She was bundled in a white winter coat and red hat and gloves, carrying a bag, and I couldn't see her face.

"Someone's early," Mason said.

Beck squinted. "Can't see her, too far away."

Pia's guest's face came into view.

I froze.

Mason and Beck kept walking for a few seconds but then stopped too, looking back at me. It was the pharmacist I'd been meaning to ask the guys about.

"Hey, Delaney," Mason said as she reached us.

Delaney. *This* was Pia's friend Delaney? The one I'd been hearing about for months? My mind raced, trying to remember everything Mason had said.

Moved here in... maybe high school? Moved away. Boyfriend. Breakup. Came back. Another breakup. Holy shit, the redheaded pharmacist was Delaney.

"Hey, guys."

We already dated.

Beck had said that about her at one point. Fuck.

She was looking at me.

"Let me take that," I said of her massive shopping bag. "It's still a little slippery."

Drawn to her, wanting any excuse to get closer, I was unusually happy to see her remove the shopping bag from her shoulder. When I took it from her, those blue/gray eyes locked with mine. There was a question behind them, but she didn't ask anything, saying simply, "Thanks."

"I'll meet you there," I called up to Mason and Beck.

An outsider to our group would never have been able to discern the look I gave them, the extremely subtle glance that said, "Don't argue with me, just go."

Without a word, both guys took the hint and kept walking.

"I don't want to hold you up," Delaney said beside me.

Adorable. It wasn't a word I used often, but one that fit her completely. She might take offense if I said it aloud. In my experience, women were more comfortable with compliments like gorgeous or stunning. Cute and adorable, one of my exes said, described puppies. Not women. But dammit, she was... all bundled up like that.

"We're just heading to Cedarwood. I'll catch up."

"You guys were kicked out tonight?" she asked, amusement in her voice.

I opened the front door to the house portion of the inn. "Unceremoniously."

Her laugh. Goddammit, now that was a sound I could get used to.

"Thanks for coming early." Pia came from the kitchen, stopping when she saw me.

"Just helping with her bag. I wouldn't dream of interrupting girls' night."

Delaney took the bag back from me. "Thanks for carrying it in."

"No problem."

"I guess you two already met in the driveway?"

"Sort of," I said. "She can explain."

Pia looked back and forth between us. I hadn't meant that to sound so conspiratorial.

"Have fun, ladies." As much as I didn't want to leave, it was time to go. Delaney was watching me, but I couldn't pinpoint her expression. It wasn't interest, unfortunately. More like curiosity.

"Thanks again," she said, disappearing back into the kitchen with Pia.

I stood there a few seconds more, thinking back. How *was* it possible we'd never met? When exactly did she move back to Cedar Falls? Since Pia had arrived in the fall, I'd heard Delaney's name. I thought about the events at Heritage Hill. The New Year's Eve party. Was she still dating the ex then? He was from out of town, and I remembered Pia saying she visited him a lot. But still, that she and Pia were so close and this was the first time we'd run into each other...

Realizing I was still standing in the entranceway, I headed back out. Into the cold. Knowing the second I got to Cedarwood the questions would come. Being around her a few more minutes, carrying Delaney's bag, would come with a price.

One I'd gladly pay.

7

DELANEY

"What is it?"

Holy shitballs. "Nothing."

"I know you better than that," Pia said, putting chips into a bowl. "Something is definitely up."

It was him. VitalFlow guy was Parker. Mason's Parker.

"Nothing," I repeated, unloading my own bag.

We were in the kitchen, getting ready for the others. Pia, unfortunately, was watching me, knowing I'd lied through my teeth. I couldn't tell her, confidentiality and all. But she knew something was up.

So I said the next best thing that also happened to be true.

"Parker is cute."

"Duh. I told you that already. Probably the next cutest of the four of them, besides Mason. Actually, Cole's pretty hot, in a Clark Kent-ish kinda way. And Beck is... Beck."

I got what she was saying. If you didn't know Beck, he was probably the most classically good-looking of them all, excluding Cole who I'd never met. But the fact that Beck dated every woman in Cedar Falls, plus most of the pretty tourists that came through in his preferred age range, dulled the whole hot-factor thing.

"He looks a little like a cowboy. Not that I've ever met a cowboy, but that's what I'd imagine one looks like. Strong jaw. Very rugged looking, you know?"

If I was talking fast, it was to convince Pia that was all there was to it. A cute guy sighting. Nothing more, or less.

I peeked at her just as Pia poured two wines. She was anything but convinced.

"It's the boots," she said. "You're acting weird."

"Maybe it's just because I haven't seen a guy that attractive in a while. So soon after Makis and all."

The last thing I wanted to talk about was Makis. Even now, saying his name gave me a huge pit in my stomach and reminded me that it had been, what? Like two hours since I last thought of him? When would this guy freaking leave my brain?

"Uh huh."

"What?" I deflected.

Pia leaned against the kitchen counter, sipping her wine. "It's funny, isn't it? That you guys never met before."

Double damn. I really didn't want to lie to Pia, but I also wasn't a fan of breaking the law either. "Fine," I said, about to smack myself. I didn't have to say what he'd come in for. "We did meet already. He came in for a prescription the other day."

Not surprisingly, Pia was immediately suspicious. "And you didn't tell me, because?"

Excellent question. "HIPPA and privacy and all that."

"Right. But I didn't ask what he came in for. You could have mentioned you guys met. I'm surprised he didn't say anything to Mason either. That I know of."

I nearly spit out my wine. "I don't think we introduced

ourselves so he probably didn't know who I was." Also, there was very little chance he'd broadcast what he came in for.

"So let's hear it."

Sighing, I said honestly, "I panicked when I saw him, not wanting to share too much. That's all."

"It's not like he came in for some life-sustaining drug and you..." Pia stopped. Her eyes widened. "Did he... Is Parker..."

"No," I assured her. "It's nothing like that."

The fact that I was able to remain straight-faced at the thought of telling Pia what he'd actually come in for made me wonder if maybe I could be an actress. It wasn't a career I'd ever considered before, but maybe a viable career path? Since my day job wasn't all it was cracked up to be.

"So you met Parker, didn't tell me, and think he's cute. Did I miss anything?"

"Nope," I said, too quickly. "Nothing at all."

Pia put down her wine and continued getting snacks ready, stirring a bowl of what looked like dip. "He also happens to be extremely nice, adventurous, charming... and single."

"That's where I have to stop you," I said, sincere. "When I say I'm not interested in dating anytime soon, I'm not interested. For real."

"Who said anything about dating?"

"Pia," I admonished. "Are you suggesting I sleep with Mason's friend just for the sake of—"

"Having some good sex to clear your mind of that giant asshole? Sure am."

"You just said yourself, he's a nice guy. Doesn't seem to be the Beck-type at all, if you know what I mean."

"I know exactly what you mean, but that doesn't preclude him from having sex with women he doesn't intend to marry."

"Bachelor pact and all?"

"Exactly. We were just talking about that the other day. Parker... has his reasons to be single too."

I was about to ask what those reasons were until I remembered the feeling of utter and complete emptiness, of rejection and humiliation, when Makis broke up with me for the second time. And that was after I'd told myself, the first time, I'd never let it happen again.

So I didn't ask. Didn't care.

"Good reasons, I bet. The guy's got it right. Dating sucks. Zero stars. Do not recommend."

"Oh, stop, you don't mean that."

"I swear on..." Thinking about that for a second, I said, "I swear on a tuna sandwich I mean it, 100 percent."

"Who swears on a tuna sandwich?"

"I do. With little bits of celery, on toast, to be specific."

"How in the world you don't like fish but you do like canned tuna is one of life's big mysteries for me."

Laughing, I grabbed the veggie tray as Pia spooned dip into a small bowl. "What else can I bring out there?"

"If I didn't know you better, I'd think you were changing the subject."

"The chip bowl? Got it."

Ignoring Pia's frown, I carried both out of the kitchen, congratulating myself on successfully changing the subject.

Parker's secret was safe with me.

8

PARKER

With the day off, I'd planned to work at the inn but Mason put the kibosh on that idea. Most of my spare time in the past few months had been taken up with renovating Heritage Hill, and apparently he and Pia had decided it was time for a break. We'd take the next few weeks off and jump in after Valentine's Day. Typically the winter months were slower for tourism, but mid-February was an exception.

Unlike Beck, who had a constant desire to stay busy, I relished a slow day with no responsibilities. Hitting the gym early, I headed back to shower and considered texting a buddy of mine for some ice fishing when I entered the kitchen and heard Pia talking.

"Can't, sorry. I'm meeting Delaney for lunch."

"Speaking of Delaney." Mason smiled at me.

Fucker.

"Not in the mood," I said. "Morning, Pia."

"Morning. Coffee's fresh."

"Thanks." I headed to the coffee pot. "Beck still sleeping?"

"Yep." Mason pulled out a carton of eggs. "Scrambled with cheese. Interested?"

"Esther didn't cook today?"

Typically she made breakfast in the second kitchen which we'd renovated after the holidays. Now that Heritage Hill was hosting parties, and weddings soon, it had been industrially retrofitted, which Esther didn't love. Like Mason's dad, she hadn't wanted anything to change, but that was how Heritage Hill had fallen by the wayside in the first place.

"No guests this weekend," Mason said, obviously not pleased by the fact.

"It's the only one," Pia pointed out. "And by next winter we'll have a plan in place for the slower months. Baby steps," she said as I poured my coffee.

Mason grunted.

"I'll have two," I said as Mason began cracking eggs. "No cheese though."

"Duh."

"I swear the two of you sound like twelve-year-olds sometimes."

I flashed Pia a grin. "Only sometimes?"

"Back to Delaney." Mason whisked the eggs the exact same way I'd seen Esther do it a hundred times. "Did you hear our two lovebirds met before yesterday?"

"I did." Pia peeked up at me above her coffee mug. "Funny she didn't mention it before last night."

"I must have made one hell of an impression," I said wryly, remembering last night when I'd gotten to the bar. Mason and Beck made a huge show of pretending to be Delaney and me, me asking if I could carry her bag. I smiled at the memory of Beck acting like a woman.

"Actually," she hedged. I looked up. "You did."

"Go on," Mason prompted, saving me from having to sound too eager since I'd been about to say the same thing.

"There's nothing to tell. She thought you were cute, that's all."

"Cute?" Mason sounded less than pleased about the description.

"Maybe that's not the word she used."

"So what word did she use?"

Mason was one hell of a wingman. I listened to their exchange, not saying a word.

"I can't go spilling all my secrets," Pia said, addressing me. "Sorry, Parker. Girl code and all."

"No worries," I assured her, playing it cool.

But Pia was no dummy. She watched me closely. "Do you have lunch plans?"

"No," I said as Pia jumped up from her stool to make toast. "I was thinking of ice fishing."

Pia wrinkled her nose. "That sounds horrible. Sorry, Park. But sitting on the ice, in the cold, waiting for hours to catch a fish?" She shivered.

"It's not for everyone," I agreed, getting up myself to grab three plates.

"If your plans aren't set in stone, maybe you could meet Delaney instead? She has an hour break."

"Pia," Mason warned. "Maybe we shouldn't get involved."

She brushed off Mason's warning. "You're not. I am." Then to me. "I'll admit, if it weren't for Makis, I always thought you two would be perfect for each other."

Mason snorted. "Because Delaney loves the outdoors so much? And Parker's artsy side is so sophisticated? Sorry, Parker," he added, not sorry at all, at least judging from his tone.

Holding out my plate for eggs before Mason drowned them

in cheese, I headed to the toaster to wait. "Okay, so they're a little different," Pia said to me. "But in the ways that count, you two are so alike. Two of the nicest people I know who see the bright side to things. Delaney is big on positive vibes, and I know you're all about that sort of thing."

She wasn't wrong.

No sense getting your panties in a bunch for things you couldn't control. I learned that early on in life. Might as well find the silver lining.

"And also, she's really pretty, don't you think?"

More than really pretty, but hell if I'd admit that to Pia. Girl code and all. She'd probably text her before I finished my eggs. "Toast's up," I said, snagging one and slapping some butter on it.

"Way to change the subject," Pia accused.

"Thanks," I said, as if she'd complimented me. Mason snickered.

Sitting back down, considering Pia's offer, I probed a bit. "How is it possible we never met before now?"

"Well," Pia said, "she only moved back to Cedar Falls just before I came to town. And got back with Makis when we really started hanging out more. So she was either working or heading to Clearwater on days off."

"Didn't he ever come to Cedar Falls? Seems like an awful lot of driving to me?"

"Are you kidding me? That would have made her life easier, and Makis was all about one person. Makis. I swear the guy is a full-blown narcissist."

"Sounds charming," I said as Pia and Mason sat down to eat. "What did she see in him?"

"Good question. I think he laid it on thick at the beginning and by the time Delaney started seeing bits of the real him, it was too late. She knew some of his bullshit was unacceptable, and they did break up once and nearly a half dozen other times, but it was like he had some kind of spell on her."

"I know guys like him," Mason said. His time deployed in the military, and as an NYPD cop, meant he had all sorts of experience with people. Some of the stories he'd told over the years made the hair on my neck stand up straight. "They turn on the charm, mirror their victims to present an idealized version of themselves that doesn't really exist. Real assholes."

"That sounds about right," Pia said after finishing a mouthful of eggs. "Although victim may be a little harsh."

"It's not," Mason said. Apparently it was all he would add to the topic. Digging into his breakfast, the man of many words had spoken and now he would concentrate on his food. They often teased Mason he was so good at compartmentalizing everything, including conversations, his decision to become an Army Ranger made total sense.

I, on the other hand, was convinced I had undiagnosed ADHD. It was one of the reasons I liked working with my hands and keeping busy. The only exception was fishing, but even my father agreed I wasn't the most patient fisherman on the planet, which was why I did it so often. Practice made perfect.

"Soooo," Pia said, likely circling back. "Delaney. Lunch?"

"You really think that's a good idea?" I asked. I'd admit the thought of seeing her today, having a conversation with her, was more than a little appealing. "All things considered?"

Mason watched us carefully, but said nothing.

"Things? Such as?" Pia asked.

"The fact that neither of us are looking for a relationship. At least, I imagine after going through the wringer, it's not high on her list."

Bingo. It didn't matter what Pia said, her expression gave away the fact that I was right.

"I'll admit she's more into work, gym, and girls' nights at the moment. She really has gone through the wringer so I think it would be good for her."

"Care to define 'it'?" Mason asked.

Pia frowned. "You know. Getting back in the saddle."

I raised my brows, more to tease Pia than anything else.

"Which saddle would that be?" Mason, as always, was relentless.

"Oh my God, the two of you are going to get it."

To let her off the hook, and because I was genuinely attracted to her friend, I agreed. "Give me a time and place."

Pia's eyes widened. "You're going to meet her?"

"Yeah. But I think you should give her the heads up."

"Sure," Pia agreed. "We'd planned to meet at The Coffee Cabin at noon."

Mason and I exchanged a glance. He didn't need to say a word. And to be honest, I agreed with him. This might not be the best idea, getting involved with Pia's friend. But she didn't seem to mind, knowing my aversion to long-term commitments. What was there to lose? I also didn't plan to stay a monk for the rest of my life either.

"Tell Delaney I'll see her at noon."

9

DELANEY

> BTW, forgot to mention. Can't make lunch. A friend of mine is taking my place.

It was two minutes to noon. Why did Pia wait until now to tell me she couldn't meet? And who was her friend? It was beyond strange, but with a half a block to The Coffee Cabin, not much I could do about it now.

> A friend of yours?

It couldn't be Jules. She'd have just said that. Most of our friends were mutual ones, so who the heck was she talking about?

I opened the door, eager to get out of the cold.

Looking around, I didn't see anyone who might be a friend of...

No flipping way.

He stood.

I inadvertently looked... there. How embarrassing. Had he

seen me glancing down at his crotch? And what exactly was I looking for? I never did such a thing. Geez Louise.

He was dressed casually, jeans and an olive-green sweater that made him look like he could be on the cover of some outdoor men's magazine. Neither Mason nor Beck had a thing on this guy. He was, by far, the hottest of all three.

I made my way to the table.

The Coffee Cabin was one of those places in town that was always busy. From morning to late afternoon, when they closed in the winter, it was packed. Somehow he'd found a seat for two in the corner.

"She didn't tell you?"

Obviously I wasn't able to hide my look of surprise very well.

"If a text two minutes ago without any indication of who I would be meeting counts, then actually, she did," I said, assuming he referred to Pia.

Taking off my gloves and coat, I shoved the former inside my jacket sleeves and slung it on the back of a chair.

"If you'd rather not—"

"No," I said, stopping him. "It's totally fine. I was actually telling Pia," I said, sitting down as he did the same, "it's surprising we haven't run into each other yet."

What did it mean that he was here for lunch? Was this like... a date? I hoped not because I was a long—very, very long—way away from being ready to date.

A guy this good-looking though? You sure about that, Delaney?

Then, of course, there was his little problem...

"Agreed," he said. "But Pia's going to get it. I specifically told her to make sure it was okay with you that I take her place."

"You know she'll argue that she did, and that technically she was in the right."

"Oh, I do. Pia doesn't intimidate easily."

"Could you imagine Mason with someone who did?" I asked.

His smile would make a dentist proud. "Not at all. So what can I get you? Need a menu?"

"You don't have to—"

"I insist."

Shit. If he was buying lunch, that made it more like a date. Which this definitely was not. But what was I supposed to say? "If you insist." I smiled. "Tuna on a croissant, unsweetened iced tea."

"The woman knows what she wants," he said, standing.

"If they serve tuna, I'm getting it. End of story."

Again, that smile. "I don't think I've ever met anyone who was such a fan. Tuna is usually one of those, 'Sure, I like it' but not a 'Best ever' kind of food."

"I get that a lot. Even stranger, I don't like any other seafood."

Most people had something to say about the fact that I liked tuna, from a can only, but not seafood, but Parker didn't miss a beat. "Like I said, the woman knows what she likes. I'll be right back."

I watched him head to the counter to order and nearly forgot that I'd intended to text Pia, distracted by his very fine-looking ass.

> I'm going to kill you.

Thankfully, I didn't have to wait long for her reply, which came in the form of an angel emoji. Apparently, that was all she planned to text.

> Uh huh. I'm. Not. Dating. Yet.

Think of it as lunch with me.

Except, you are not six foot something with sandy brown hair, a chiseled jaw and perfect smile.

I didn't mention his fine ass.

I don't have a perfect smile?

Cheeky girl. Ignoring her question, I texted:

He's coming back. TTYL.

"I didn't know if you wanted any sweetener," Parker said, putting down the tray of food and drinks in front of us. "So I grabbed a few of each kind."

That was thoughtful. "Thanks," I said. "And thank you for lunch."

"My pleasure."

"So how exactly did you get roped into this?" I asked, noticing his eyes for the first time. Hazel, though slightly more green than blue, probably thanks to his sweater. They were kind eyes, but I wasn't so easily fooled.

Makis had seemed kind too, in the beginning.

"Roped isn't the right word." Parker opened his bottle of water.

"No?" I teased. "So what word would you use?" I regretted the words as soon as they flew out of my mouth. Much too flirty.

The corners of Parker's lips lifted ever so slowly, his eyes mischievous. "More like, cajoled."

Laughing, I put the lid back on my iced tea after sufficiently sugaring it. "That's just as bad. Maybe even worse."

"Hmm." He took a bite of what looked like a turkey sandwich.

"A very convenient time not to be able to respond."

Parker smiled even as he chewed. I took the opportunity to dig into my own sandwich.

"Pia probably could sense I was going stir-crazy," he said when he finished. "It's rare for me to have a day off, between my regular job and working at the inn."

"I've seen the updates you made. The place looks great. It's really nice of you to do that."

"I am staying there rent-free," Parker said, taking another bite of his sandwich.

"Right, but Pia told me Mason said you're doing it more out of convenience, to help with renovations whenever you have a break."

"The inn needed renovating," he said. "Plus, when it's done I'll be able to use the job on my resume. I'm hoping to start my own construction company. Maybe," he added.

"Why maybe?"

"It's... complicated." He cocked his head to the side. "But speaking of the inn, it's still hard to believe you've been there, and we never ran into each other."

"Well, we did the other day. And I've only been down there one other time since meeting Pia. Aside from years ago, of course. But that doesn't count."

"You weren't at the New Year's Eve party?"

"No," I said. "My ex..." I stopped, not wanting to talk about Makis.

"Pia told me a little about him. Moving on." He smiled good-naturedly. But I couldn't let the opportunity pass me by.

"Then she probably told you I'm not dating yet either.

Maybe ever." I laughed, trying to make light of it, but it sounded forced. Even to me.

"She did." He gestured toward us and the table of half-eaten food. "This isn't a date. No pressure at all. Just me getting to know a friend of a friend."

Now why did that feel almost disappointing?

Knock it off, Delaney. You don't want this to be a date.

"It is crazy that we haven't crossed paths before. Until last week," I clarified. And because I was sometimes awkward as all hell, I decided to blurt out the other remaining elephant in the room. "By the way, your secret is safe with me. I would never tell anyone about a customer's medication. Just in case you were worried about that."

Parker looked genuinely confused.

"The one you came to pick up," I clarified. "Last week. When we met."

"Oh, I remember," he said, his tone slightly suggestive. He sat back then, as if something had occurred to him. "What medication was it, exactly, that my dad had me picking up?"

My dad.

Had he just said... my dad?

Oh, shit.

"It was for Parker Scott," I said, remembering the name on the order.

"Right. Also my dad's name. I'm a junior."

The medication wasn't for him. I broke out into a laugh, unable to contain it. He probably thought I was looney tunes. "Oh my God, I can't even."

"Delaney?"

I shook my head. "I'm sorry. I can't say. Confidentiality and all. But I did... think it was for you."

The poor guy was genuinely confused now. He made a face

that said, "Come on, tell me." I motioned that my lips were sealed, trying desperately not to burst out laughing again.

Parker pulled out his phone. Fired off a text.

"Texting your dad?"

"Yeah," he said, taking a bite of his sandwich.

I'd have done the same but wasn't confident that tuna wouldn't end up splattered all over the table when I started laughing again. I simply could not stop smiling.

"I'm guessing it wasn't his cholesterol medication?"

I shook my head.

Parker looked back down to his phone, which was on the table. Apparently his dad was a quick texter. Hopefully the son took after him. I hated slow texters.

Not that it mattered.

It was impossible to read his face, Parker half smiling and half looking like he might toss his phone across the room.

"I'm gonna kill him."

Parker and I locked gazes.

I pressed my lips together.

"All this time you thought... that I..."

Nodding, I did take a drink then, mostly just to cover my face. There was a 100 percent chance my cheeks were flaming red.

"No wonder you don't want to date me."

He said it so matter-of-factly, with zero bitterness and laughter in his voice, that I could not resist a reply.

"That actually has nothing to do with it," I said after swallowing a big gulp of iced tea. "Seriously. If I were to go on a date with anyone, honestly, it would be you."

Maybe a little too much honesty? But it was true.

Sure, the "nice guy" thing could be a facade, but Pia knew him well. And he'd been friends with Mason a long time. I'd heard Parker referred to as "the nice one" before, and it seemed to be with good reason.

He was also hot, easy-going, had a nice ass, was funny, and did I mention seriously freaking hot?

"Oh, man." He shook his head. "I still can't believe this one." Parker smiled. "You might have pharmacist/patient confidentiality, but thankfully, I don't and can't wait to tell the guys this one."

"You would out your father like that?"

"Abso-fucking-lutely. Sorry for the swearing," he said immediately.

"No apologies necessary. I have a potty mouth too."

"Don't think poorly of me, but my father has been a pain in the ass for as long as I can remember. This is very much on brand for him, and the guys won't even be a little surprised. The fact that he couldn't go one weekend without it," he sighed. "Dad met a woman the night before at O'Malley's."

"Pia mentioned your parents were divorced."

"Yeah. Unbelievable." He shook his head. "It's too bad this isn't a date. Would have been one hell of a first one."

Seemed like he didn't want to talk about the parents, which was okay by me. "It really would have been," I admitted, oddly relieved the medication was actually his father's.

Which made no sense since this wasn't a date.

Because I was no longer dating.

Such a shame...

10

PARKER

When I'd gotten back from lunch, Mason was nowhere to be found. I tracked down Pia, who was in her office with no idea where her fiancé had gone off to. When she asked about lunch, I laughed, asking if she'd talked to Delaney yet. Pia admitted her friend had texted when she was finished, but Pia had been on a work call that had just ended.

I told her to call Delaney immediately and left a bewildered Pia behind.

"Hey, buddy." I found Beck in the kitchen. "Have you seen Mason?"

"No, why?"

"Pop Tarts? Are you ten?"

Beck pulled the tarts out of the toaster. "These things are damn good. Want one?"

I pulled a water from the fridge. "I'll pass. Thought you gave them up when you lost your abs?"

"First of all, I didn't lose my abs. Not all of them, at least." Beck took a bite.

"And second of all?"

He finished chewing. "Second of all, I never intended to give them up forever."

Beck loved Pop Tarts almost as much as he loved women.

"Third of all, when you start wearing matching socks, I'll stop eating Pop Tarts."

"They match," I said of my socks. "You just can't tell."

Beck didn't comment. I couldn't even remember how the crazy socks started, but they became a *thing* in college. Being known for them was as good a talking point as any, and people —girls in particular—started buying them for me. So of course, I had to wear them.

"Got these in my Easter basket last year," I said.

"The fact that you get an Easter basket at your age is disturbing."

"Says the guy eating Pop Tarts for breakfast because he probably just woke up despite the fact that it's after one in the afternoon."

"Late night," he muttered between bites.

"I was with you, dipshit."

"I can hear the two of you bickering like an old married couple," Mason said, walking into the kitchen, "halfway down the hall." He looked at Beck's choice of breakfast food and rolled his eyes.

"What? Your fiancée got them for me," Beck argued.

"Of course she did."

Pia adored Beck, so that made sense. "It's ironic that she sees through your bullshit but still likes you so much."

"Fuck off."

"Speaking of fucking," I said, eager to tell the guys this one. "I had lunch with Delaney today."

"You what?" Beck asked.

I filled him in on how that ended up happening. "More

importantly, you'll never believe this one. Even for my father, it's a doozy."

Mason leaned back against the kitchen counter, crossed his arms, and waited.

Beck, eyes wide, finished off his Pop Tart.

"So he asked me to stop at the pharmacy last weekend when he was in town, which is where I first met Delaney."

"Delaaaaney." Beck said her name in a sing-song voice, like a three-year-old might. The guy was addicted to hearing the sound of his voice.

"I didn't think to look at the medication, but apparently Dad has been having some difficulty getting it up." I let that sink in before adding, "So I had no idea she thought the meds were for me this whole time."

"Oh." Mason broke into a huge grin. "That's rich."

"And she still had lunch with you?" Beck laughed. "Your fucking father is a real winner."

"When you say 'fucking father' do you mean that literally, or..." Mason laughed at his own joke.

"Funny," I said. "Can you believe the guy?"

"Yes, we can," Mason said. "What amazes me is how opposite the two of you are."

"Thankfully, I got most of my mother's genes." Though I wasn't taking any chances, just in case being a major dickhead after the nuptials was also an inherited trait.

"That's not how it works," Beck said, wiping crumbs from his breakfast onto the floor, earning a stern look from Mason. "You get half of your genes from each parent."

"It was a figure of speech," I pointed out.

"A figure of speech," Mason said in his best Professor Cole voice, "is a non-literal word or phrase used for rhetorical effect."

"Is that what it is?" Beck asked in his best smartass voice.

"Does Pia know about this?" Mason asked.

"Speak of the devil," I said as Pia walked in.

"Know about what?" she asked.

"You didn't talk to Delaney yet?" I asked.

"I just did."

"So she didn't tell you?"

"About lunch?"

"About my father."

Mason and Beck watched the two of us as if it were a tennis match. Pia shook her head.

When I told Pia what happened, her eyes widened.

"She would never tell me." Pia stifled a smile. "Delaney takes confidentiality with her patients very seriously."

"Obviously it doesn't leave this room."

"Your dad's dick is not typically a topic of conversation at the bar," Beck said. "But if it comes up, I'll be sure not to mention it to anyone."

"Are you working tonight?" Pia asked him.

"Is the sky blue?"

"At the moment." She peeked out the kitchen window, Heritage Hill's lakeside view one of its best features. At the moment, Pia was apparently noticing the very gray skies typical of late January in the Finger Lakes. "No. It's not."

That Mason's fiancée so easily fit into our group was just one of the many reasons we all liked her so much.

"Delaney is off at six," Pia said to Mason. "It's still weird for her to be around on the weekend, so Jules and I were thinking to re-acclimate her to Saturday night in Cedar Falls. Maybe The Grapevine for dinner, Big Easy for a drink and then meet you at O'Malley's later?"

"Works for me," he said. Mason looked at me.

"I could go for some wings. Any interest in—"

"I'm on at seven," Beck cut in. "Come to O'Malley's to eat."

"Your wings are crap."

"I'll tell them extra crispy."

Mason sighed. He didn't want to eat at O'Malley's, but Beck was feeling left out. Always the mediator, I said, "We'll hit Taylor's for a wing appetizer and come over for dinner."

"I swear to God," Mason said. "You have more FOMO than—"

"If you say a girl, I'm coming after you," Pia intervened.

"Yeah? Coming after me how?" Mason got to her first, putting Pia in a bearhug which there was no escaping from. The former Army Ranger had skills that all of us, myself included, gave a wide berth around.

"So I guess you'll be seeing Delaney for the second time in a day," Pia said after Mason let her go.

"I guess so," I said, trying to sound nonchalant. "She made it clear lunch wasn't a date," I added. "So don't get that look."

"What look?"

"Mmm hmm."

"Delaney is... how do I put this... in transition."

"Transition?" Beck chuckled. "You make her sound like a vampire."

"You're not watching *True Blood* again, are you?" Pia asked him.

Beck's rare silence answered for him.

"To me," I stepped in before the two of them started a debate on the merits of watching new shows versus re-watching old ones, "it didn't sound like a transition phase but more a 'done with dating' phase."

Pia rolled her eyes. "Isn't that the same phase all four of you were supposedly in when you agreed to the pact?"

"Whoa," Beck said. "We took a bachelor pact. Not a non-dating pact. Big difference."

"Huge," Mason added.

"That's what she said," I finished, for good measure.

"Anyway." Pia pretended we hadn't spoken. "Just think of it like Delaney took the bachelor pact too. She's totally fine to date but has no interest, at the moment, in a boyfriend."

I thought back to our conversation. "She specifically said, and I quote, 'I'm not dating. Maybe ever.' Which isn't at all 'totally fine to date.'"

Pia crossed her arms. "Oh, yeah? Then why, when I asked her what you two talked about, was she not able to remember because she, and I quote, 'was too busy staring at him to think straight for half the lunch?'"

Mason and Beck made sounds that could land the two of them in a zoo if anyone overheard them. Bunch of animals. Toddler animals. Not that I was judging since I probably would have made a similar sound if we weren't talking about me.

More importantly, "She said that?"

"My lips are sealed. I've already said too much."

"A bit too late to seal them, Pia." Mason reached for her again, pulling her into his chest and wrapping his arms around her.

"Well, I'm not saying any more," she clarified. "Except that... maybe Delaney just needs to realize not all guys are assholes."

"I can—" Beck started, until all three of us said, "No," at the exact same time.

"I'm not looking for anything serious either, as you know. But I don't want to fuck around with your friend."

"Except literally," Beck said.

Everyone ignored him.

"Delaney is a big girl and can take care of herself," Pia said. "Just like you're a big boy, and I won't try to pressure you."

I would have muttered, "Too late," but that sounded way too much like Beck for my taste. Pia pushed away from Mason, reached up to kiss him on the cheek, and then headed back out of the kitchen.

But not before pausing at the door to add, "Though she did ask me if you'd be there."

With a wiggle of her fingers, Pia left.

I looked at Mason.

"Nothing I can do. She's uncontrollable. Nice socks, by the way."

I looked down, considered whether or not I should wear normal socks tonight and immediately decided not to change my style to impress a woman.

Like the lunch, it wasn't a date. Both Delaney and I were both just tagging along and would happen to be at the same bar. No big deal.

Then why did a wave of adrenaline rush through me, as if it was a big deal?

As if you don't already know the answer.

11

DELANEY

"You're wearing normal socks."

Of all the stupid things to say first. With a few vodka sodas under my belt, though, it wasn't surprising. Despite myself, I'd been tuned up all night, knowing I would see Parker again. At least I didn't say what had run through my head when we walked into O'Malley's and I first saw him. Making out with him was not on my to-do list tonight, even if I couldn't stop thinking about it.

"Every once in a while I like to mix it up."

Pia and Mason were already heading to the dance floor as Jules found someone she knew at the other end of the bar.

"Help yourself," he said of the empty seat next to him. "Mason won't be back anytime soon."

I sat. "He just doesn't seem the dancing type to me."

"Agreed. But I guess even big, tough military guys like to cut a rug every once in a while."

"Sup, Delaney?" Beck interrupted us. "What can I get you?"

"Hi, Beck. Vodka soda. Tito's, please."

"Splash of cran?"

"Sure, why not."

"Coming up."

Parker's hand wrapped around his beer bottle. His hands were big. Strong, I assumed, from working with them every day.

I swallowed, reminding myself for the umpteenth time today... no dating.

"So I hear the two of you have a history?"

Laughing, I tried to imagine what Beck had told him. "Hardly. We were"—I used air quotes—"boyfriend and girl-friend in middle school. Never even kissed. Beck," I said as my old friend delivered the vodka soda, "was too much of a chicken shit to attempt it."

"Hey," Beck said as Parker quietly tapped the money in front of him and Beck took my drink payment, "it takes two to tango, Miss Delaney."

"As if I would have ever attempted it. You know me better than that."

Beck turned to Parker. "Delaney is much too nice. She's like the female version of you, actually."

"I'd say you got off easy," Parker said to me.

"Oh, by high school, he found his groove alright. Thankfully, we just stayed friends."

"Uh," Beck said, as if wounded. "I would have made a great boyfriend."

Smiling, I pulled the drink toward me. "I think we have different definitions of what a great boyfriend is."

Beck winked and moved off to serve drinks.

"What's your definition of one?" Parker asked, still smiling.

I thought about that for a second. "Honestly? This is going to sound really negative, and I hate to be negative. It puts bad ju-ju into the universe."

"Hit me."

"A non-existent one," I said, the answer too easy.

"He was that bad?"

"Yeah," I admitted. "He was that bad. I mean, not at first, obviously."

"Tell me."

"Nah," I said as a new song started. I peeked onto the dance floor but couldn't see Pia or Mason. "I don't want to be a cliché, talking about the ex."

"Tell me," he said again. If he'd said it more firmly, the words would have sounded like a command. But his tone wasn't like that. Parker said it gently, as if he really wanted to hear.

I looked into his eyes. There was nothing there but kindness. If it was an act, it was a damn good one.

Here went nothing. "For the first few months, he was amazing. Told me everything a woman wants to hear. 'I never met anyone like you' and stuff like that. Then things began to cool off. He was busier and busier, just... didn't really prioritize our relationship. Eventually he broke up with me, and just when I was starting to feel okay, he came back. Said he'd made a mistake. And the whole thing started all over again. That's the worst of it, falling for his shit twice. I feel like a complete idiot."

"You're not an idiot. Love does funny things to people."

"That's the thing. When I think back, I don't even know if I loved him or was just addicted to him. I would think love was reciprocal, and more and more I'm realizing the only person he truly loved was himself." That was enough. No more ex talk. I changed the subject. "What about you? Have you ever been in love?"

"Twice," Parker said, quickly enough that I knew he'd given it some thought. "College girlfriend. And then again a few years later."

"So what happened?"

Parker inhaled, got a faraway look into those hazel eyes of his. "College happened, the first time. We both sort of realized it was too soon to settle down with one person. It was only junior year, and there was a lot of partying to do. It was pretty amicable, actually."

Of course it was. I had a hard time seeing Parker *not* amicable with anyone.

"The second time was a little messier. It was just after I'd moved to Cedar Falls that I met her, and we started dating. She was from Oakridge and in town wine tasting with friends when we met. Did the long-distance thing for a while, but her mother owned a dental practice there, and she was poised to take it over which meant she wasn't moving. She was ready to settle down, get engaged and all that."

"And you weren't?"

"Not sure if I'll ever be."

Ouch. "Bachelor pact and all?"

Conversation buzzed around us. Music played from the other side of the bar. But for all intents and purposes, it might as well just have been the two of us, I was so engrossed in talking to him.

"That wouldn't stop me, obviously. But I took it for a reason."

"Being?"

He'd been staring at his beer. Parker's head jolted up.

Shit. I pushed too hard. "Sorry, I didn't mean to—"

"My dad cheated. Multiple times. Tore apart my mother. Ripped up the family. Everyone was completely shocked. Mom and Dad had been the perfect couple." He frowned. "Perfect except for the fact that Dad had led a double, secret life for longer than anyone could have realized."

"Oh, man, that's awful."

"The fact that he came to town to visit and ended up"—

Parker smiled—"getting that prescription after meeting a woman out at a bar the night before?" He shrugged like it was no big deal, but I could tell it was a huge deal. "Is very… him."

"Well." I lifted my glass. "Here's to shit relationships. May we not repeat them."

Parker clinked his bottle to my glass.

"What are you guys toasting to?" Pia asked as she and Mason came up to us from behind.

"You won't like it if I told you," I said, turning in my seat. "I think I stole this from you," I said, prepared to get up.

"No, stay. We're good." Mason gestured to Beck, who came immediately over. "Round for everyone. Where's Jules?"

"Over there," I said. She stood between two women, both of whom were locals.

"No. Fucking. Way."

All of us, myself included, followed Mason's gaze toward the front of the bar.

Cole Ford.

Not surprisingly, we weren't the only ones watching him come toward us. If every single woman at the bar wasn't already looking at Beck or our group—Mason and Parker made quite a pair—they were now watching Cedar Falls' golden boy. It was an ironic nickname since he'd moved away during his freshman year. And his hair was anything but golden. Actually, he was the only one of all four of the guys with black hair and a dark pair of glasses to match.

I couldn't remember how the name started, but it had followed him through elementary and middle school. Even I knew of Cole Ford, and he was a few years ahead of me, like the others.

"You fucker," Mason said, standing as Cole reached the group.

Pia and I exchanged a glance as the guys hugged and greeted each other. Even Beck came from around the bar.

"It's like the Lost Boys," she said. "Finding each other."

They really did make quite a quartet of men.

"Hi, Pia," Cole said. His voice was low. Gravely. The kind of voice that belonged on the radio or narrating a book.

"Hi, Cole," she said back.

He looked at me. "Delaney Thorton. Good to see you."

"Same," I said. "Guess the guys didn't know you were coming in?"

"Nope." He moved to stand beside Mason as Beck returned behind the bar. "It was a last-minute thing."

"Not the first time you've surprised us last minute," Parker said. "City too boring for you? Missing Cedar Falls?"

"More to it than that. I'll tell you later."

Mason's brows drew together. He was clearly confused, and maybe a little concerned. Pia's tough guy really did have a kind heart, not that he let many people see it.

"Everything okay?" Parker asked.

Cole nodded. "Yes, sir."

"Best Scotch we have." Beck handed a drink to Parker, who handed it to Cole. "On the house."

"Guess I can't complain about the quality of O'Malley's best Scotch if it's on the house." Cole lifted his glass. "Thanks, Beck."

"Anytime."

As Cole talked to the group, Parker and I exchanged a glance. We'd been having a great conversation, even if it was on the serious side.

"Do you dance?" he mouthed, pointing to the dance floor.

It was a slow song, and as much as I wanted to continue our conversation, there was a part of me that knew having Parker's hands on me would be dangerous.

So why did my head nod?

He got up.

I followed. Ignoring Pia's look. Ignoring my racing heart. Ignoring the warning bells blaring in my head, telling me to run back to the bar, back to safety.

Before I knew it, my feet stepped onto the wooden floor in front of the band, and I was in Parker's arms.

12

PARKER

She belongs here.

Reminding myself Delaney was not interested in dating, I pushed the thought away. She might fit perfectly in my arms, and smell like the first spring breeze after a long winter, but this was nothing more than a dance between friends. Or so I'd keep telling myself.

I was thrilled to see Cole, but I also didn't want the conversation with Delaney to end.

"On a lighter note," I said as we danced, trying not to focus on how, with one tug toward me, our bodies would be flush together, "tell me about your family. Have they always lived in Cedar Falls?"

"My parents actually moved here right after they got married. They came on a wine-tasting trip with some friends and loved it. Dad is an engineer. Mom is a dentist. I have an older brother who moved to Syracuse after college, and that's pretty much it."

I almost said something about attracting dentists' daughters, but thought better of it. We'd talked plenty about our exes already, and more importantly, Delaney wouldn't take kindly to hearing about my attraction to her.

"And your career?"

"I always thought I'd follow in my mother's footsteps, having spent so much time at her work when I was younger. I took biology and chem in college to prep for dental school, or maybe even med school, but changed my mind at some point. I graduated with a chemistry degree and no idea what I actually wanted to do for a living. My mother encouraged me to apply for a PharmD program, and when I got it, I figured it was as good as anything."

"But you don't love it."

"I don't. If it were up to me, I'd have done something in the arts. Maybe started my own business or something. I love to paint, and make jewelry... stuff like that. Very impractical stuff."

"A lifetime is an awfully long time not to enjoy what you do."

"True. But I also wonder if I'd love my artsy stuff... that's what my parents call it... if I had to earn a living with it. That would be a lot of pressure and probably would take away the enjoyment of it."

Although it sounded a lot like Delaney talking herself out of making a career from what she loved, I kept my mouth shut. We weren't close enough for me to offer an opinion she hadn't asked for, and I wasn't one to talk when it came to pulling the trigger on starting a business.

"Your turn."

Unfortunately, the song ended which meant I had to let her go. The second I did, I wanted to pull her back. Instead, we walked off the dance floor, but instead of heading back to the bar, Delaney stepped off to the side.

I did the same.

"Not a lot to tell. Was born and raised in Hamlin, New York.

Met the guys freshman year at University of Rochester. Majored in business. I have two brothers who both work for my dad's car dealership, but I had no interest in that so I followed Mason and Beck back to Cedar Falls, started working construction, which I'd done a lot of back home while I figured things out. And here we are."

"Pia said you're a big outdoorsy guy?"

"I am. Love to fish, hike, ski... played ice hockey in college. Stuff like that."

"You're obviously still in great shape. Do you go to a gym?"

I couldn't resist. "How can you tell?"

Her eyes meandered down to my chest but immediately popped back up to my face. I'd have to remember to wear tighter shirts around Delaney.

"Are you fishing for a compliment, Parker?" she teased.

"Damn straight I am."

Delaney's tinkling laugh made me smile. "I'm sure you get plenty and don't need one from me."

Pushing my luck, I said, "What makes you so sure?"

"Haha, there you go again."

"What?" I asked with mock indignation. "I have no idea what you're talking about."

"Uh huh."

"Crap. We're being summoned."

I turned back to the bar. Her friend Jules had rejoined the group, and it looked like they were all poised to do a shot. We were, indeed, being summoned. As much as I enjoyed having Delaney to myself, we headed back.

"What are we toasting to?" I asked, keeping the mood light, knowing at least one of the guys was likely to make a smartass comment about Delaney and me lingering on the dance floor.

"Cole finally quit being so mysterious and told us why he's

home. A professor friend of his gave him the keys to his ski chalet. We're going tomorrow."

That made absolutely no sense.

"Drink first," Cole said, handing me a shot glass. "Ask later."

Pia gave Delaney one too.

"To well-connected friends." Mason lifted his glass. "And friends, in general."

"Cheers," everyone toasted. I didn't turn around to watch Delaney even though I wanted to. I'd pushed it already, asking her to dance.

"Alright," I said to Cole, "what's going on?"

"A colleague came to find me this morning in my office with the strangest request. He owns a house at Crystal Peak and is apparently having some workers come to take a look Monday morning. Apparently the property management company came out for a routine inspection and found some roof damage to the garage, probably happened during that big storm last month. He arranged to have it looked at Monday morning and planned to be there, but something came up. I don't have classes Monday so I told him I'd go up, maybe stop here and drag a few of you assholes with me." Cole smiled. "The guy's loaded. Wife's family. Doesn't need to work but..." He shrugged.

"Say no more," I said. "Odd professor types. I get it."

"Which means what, exactly?" Cole asked.

"That you're a bunch of weirdos," Mason said.

I peeked to the side. Delaney was huddled with Pia and Jules at the bar.

"You guys off tomorrow?" Cole asked us.

"I'm forcing him to step back for a few weeks with inn renovations," Mason said. "Otherwise Parker would work himself to the bone."

"It's true," I said. "He fired me."

Mason laughed. Something he did more and more often these days. When he first came home in the fall when his dad died, it had been awful. To everyone's surprise, innkeeping had been good for the former cop.

Or more like Pia had been good for him. Maybe both.

"I didn't fire you," Mason pointed out. "Hard to fire someone who works for free."

"So you're off tomorrow?" Mason asked. "Can you get off Monday too?"

I never took days so it shouldn't be a problem. "I can arrange it. What about you?" I asked Mason, who immediately turned to Pia.

"All are welcome," Cole said. "It's a huge house, apparently."

Mason smiled. "Pia, girl? Wanna hit the slopes tomorrow? We can have Esther hold down the fort for the day, and there are no guests Monday."

She turned to the group. "And be stuck alone with you clowns? Only if my girls can come," she said to Jules and Delaney.

"I'm out," Jules said. "I have a class tomorrow and deadline on an article I'm behind on. Rain check me."

It was too bad she couldn't make it, but the one person I was most interested in coming on this overnighter still hadn't said anything.

"Don't leave me hanging," Pia said to Delaney. "I know you're off Monday."

"Right," she said. "But not sure what I can do about tomorrow. I'm opening."

"What time do you work until?" I asked.

"Supposed to be until three, but maybe if I can't get the whole day I can at least get out early. I'll see what I can do."

"I was planning to hit the slopes for the day," Mason said. "Beck is off tomorrow too."

Every strike brings me closer to the next home run.

Alright, Babe Ruth, let's see which one it'll be. A strike or home run.

"I'll wait for you," I said. "I can work in the morning, and whenever you're ready, we'll leave and meet the gang there."

Ignoring Mason's small smile, and Pia's too, I waited to see how badly Delaney didn't want to date again. She was attracted to me, for sure. And I sure as hell was attracted to her too. But that didn't necessarily mean much, especially given her situation.

She looked between me and Pia, as if trying to decide.

"But that'll kill your skiing day," she said. "By the time we get there—"

"Doesn't matter. I don't ski."

She laughed. "That is a bold-face lie."

Nabbed. "True," I admitted. "But honestly, it's not a big deal."

"Come on," Pia urged. "It'll be so much fun."

"There's a hot tub," Mason said, obviously picking up the vibes.

I'd thank him later.

"How can I resist a hot tub?" she asked. "You sure you don't mind?"

Our eyes locked.

There was a shift between us, as if we'd just crossed over into new territory.

"Not at all," I said.

"OK. I'm in."

"This will be so much fun." Pia took out her phone. "I'll start a list. We'll need wine, obviously. Hot cocoa and Baileys, for the hot tub. Maybe I'll grab some bagels and cream cheese for Monday morning. We'll probably be eating out tomorrow night, right?"

"Woah, slow down, ghost rider," Mason said. "It's only one night."

"Right." Pia kept putting things into her phone. "But we're gonna make it an epic night."

After tonight, getting to know Delaney more, I'd begun to hope that maybe there was some wiggle room in her thinking on the "not dating" thing. Because being stuck in a ski chalet with her for two days, and not touching her at all, was going to be all but impossible.

I'd take a first kiss with Delaney Thorton over skiing any day.

13

DELANEY

This was nuts.

I'd sworn off dating, and men, about as well as I'd stayed away from Makis even after I knew our relationship was toxic. *He* was toxic.

Parker is not. He's one of the good guys.

That was what Pia had said last night after we danced. Apparently she and Jules had decided the two of us were perfect together and had, in Pia's words, "amazing chemistry." Not that I denied it. I'd wanted nothing more than to find myself in a dark corner of the bar making out with him.

Yet there was a part of me, a huge part of me, that wasn't the same after Makis. Healing from that relationship had not been easy. I was just finding some hard-wrought peace from dreams that had haunted me for months.

Did I really want to do it all over again?

No. The answer was no. I didn't.

And yet here I was, dragging my duffle bag down the stairs, about to get in a car for an hour—not to mention stay overnight

—with a guy who I'd spent the better part of last night, and this morning, thinking about.

Stupid. Delaney, you are stupid, stupid, stupid.

Knowing he would be here any minute, I grabbed my coat and purse, locked up and headed out onto the porch. Just about to put on my coat, Parker's pickup truck pulled up. Even if he hadn't stopped in front of my house, I'd have known the silver truck was his. It fit him perfectly.

Kind of like his jeans. Or that light green, form-fitting long-sleeved shirt he'd had on last night which didn't hide the fact that Parker worked out.

Jumping out of his truck, Parker jogged onto my porch, reaching out his hand.

"Hey there," he said as I gave him my duffle bag.

"Thanks for waiting." I followed him to the truck. And of course he opened my door, waited for me to get in, and shut it for me. That was what all guys did at first. And then a few weeks later, there'd be no more door openings. A few months later, he would take ten hours to text back. And so on from there.

I knew the drill.

"No problem," he said, tossing my bag in the small back seat. "I was surprised you could get out so early."

"I've been putting in a lot of extra hours," I said, glad not to have messed Parker up too much. It was not even noon now. "The boss used to split time with me until his son got his pharmacy license. Now he just fills in here and there. Like today."

"Glad it worked out," he said.

It was impossible not to notice how good he smelled, like musk and cedar.

Talking to Parker was so easy. For almost an hour, we chatted about work and things we liked to do and our favorite foods. We moved from one topic to the next effortlessly. I couldn't help a wave of disappointment seeing the rolling hills east of Seneca Lake that served a small ski town which I hadn't been to in years.

Like last night, I enjoyed time alone with him and wished it could be extended. All while knowing it was good to be with the group, which kept me from doing something foolish. Like accidentally kissing Parker. He'd been giving off enough of a vibe for me to tell the difference between friendzone and... what was happening between us. Kissing would not be off the table.

"According to the directions, the house is up there," he said as the truck began to climb a hill. There didn't seem to be many other houses on the road, which was thick with trees on both sides.

"Holy shit," I said, seeing it for the first time. "A log cabin."

"A huge log cabin," he clarified.

"I love them," I admitted. "But don't think I ever stayed in one."

"One of the first houses I built was a log cabin," Parker said, pulling his truck into the massive driveway. "I've done a few over the years and really enjoy them. There's actually a weekend workshop in Rochester I've been thinking of taking, specifically for log cabin builders."

"That makes sense," I said, marveling at this one. "That it would be a specialized thing."

The deck on the second floor went around the entire house. I could see the hot tub in the corner just before the deck wrapped around to the right. Part of me wanted to go explore and see the view, but it was freezing.

"Damn, it's cold," I said, attempting the door code a second time. Cole had sent it in a group text earlier.

"Your jacket," Parker pointed out, "might do more good on your body."

Finally, the code worked. "I hate being in a car with my jacket on," I said, pushing open the door. "Oh, my…"

It was incredible. To my left, an open space with couches and a stone fireplace that went two floors up to the ceiling. In front of me, the biggest kitchen I'd ever seen in my life with an informal dining area off to the left. The most striking thing wasn't the size of the place but the fact that it was a log cabin, which gave it an instant woodsy and cozy feel despite the fact that it was basically a mansion.

"Wow."

Parker was looking toward the dining area, and I could see why. Heading that way myself, my mouth dropped even further down to the floor. An entire wall of sliding glass doors and carpet-to-ceiling windows revealed the view. It was a perfect shot of the ski mountain with nothing but trees in front of it to spoil it.

"What did Cole say his friend did for a living?" I asked as Parker moved up beside me.

"A fellow professor, but he also mentioned something about the wife coming from money."

"Makes sense. This is not a college professor's house."

"Agreed. This view alone is worth millions."

We stood there for a few more seconds, our proximity hard to ignore. If I shifted just a little bit to my left, we'd be touching.

I swallowed and walked to the kitchen island.

"There's a note," I said, picking it up. The gang had already said they would be on the slopes, and we planned to join them. I read it out loud. "Welcome to the cabin! There are some hoagies and an open bottle of champagne in the fridge. Bedrooms on the third floor are yours. See you soon. xoxo, Pia and the boys."

I showed Parker.

"Pia and the boys. Sounds like a music band."

"It does. Can't argue with lunch though. I'm starved."

"Should we put our stuff away and eat?"

"Sounds like a plan."

Before I could even reach for my things, Parker had both of our duffle bags in hand. I hung my jacket on a hook near the door and followed him up the wooden staircase. The second floor boasted a landing with workout equipment that overlooked the first floor. The third floor had just two bedrooms, right across from each other.

"Take your pick," he said, peering into the first one.

"Either works for me. Actually," I said, "they look the same."

Both were decorated like the rest of the house, exactly what one would think a ski chalet in upstate New York would look like.

Parker put my bag on the bed and paused just long enough for me to register that we were in a bedroom. Our eyes met, for the briefest of seconds, before he headed out to his own room. "Will meet you downstairs in a sec," I called, heading into my own private bathroom and closing the door. I didn't need to pee, surprisingly. But I did need to breathe. Looking into the mirror, I took a few deep breaths and reminded myself of the many hours it had taken for Makis to text me back, and then most often with just a word or two. Or when he said, "I need you to access your non-crazy side" when I questioned him about the dry texting. Or the multitude of times he said I was "overthinking" which, of course, turned out not to be true since he later broke up with me.

Twice.

It had taken my friends to make me realize I hadn't done anything wrong. It was never about me. Makis simply wasn't ready for a commitment but too chicken shit to say so. Instead he strung me along and made me feel like I was losing my mind when I called him out for pulling away.

Once I was sufficiently in the right state of mind to deal with Parker—now that I no longer wanted to kiss him, knowing where that could eventually lead—I headed back downstairs.

There were two hoagies, a bag of chips and two glasses of champagne already poured. Parker picked one up and handed it to me.

"Figured nothing went better with Italian hoagies than a good champagne."

"Didn't take you for a champagne guy?"

"It was already open. How could I resist?"

"Good point." We clinked glasses. "Cheers to a surprise ski weekend with new friends."

"Cheers to that," he said.

We drank. And ate. And drank some more. By the time we were done with our second glass, I was having a hard time reclaiming the "men suck" feeling I'd managed to drum up in the bathroom.

My phone buzzed. Looking down on the counter at it, as I suspected, Pia's name popped up.

"She's wondering when we're coming," I said.

Parker had just finished clearing the counter. He looked at me. I looked at him.

Was he thinking the same thing as me? I couldn't be the one to say it. Not after making such a big deal about not dating and all that. But 100 percent of me wanted to stay here, open another bottle of something, and keep talking. He was honestly one of the easiest guys to talk to, and it felt like we were becoming fast friends.

Well, with the exception of the fact that I wanted to climb into bed with him. That part felt anything but friends to me.

"We could just go tomorrow."

Yes. Yes, yes, *yes!*

"Hmm." I pretended to think about it. "I'm not sure if the others are planning to ski tomorrow. Cole is meeting the contractor, right?"

"Yeah, he is. Up to you. I honestly am fine either way, skiing or not."

I'd ask why he was here if he didn't care about skiing, but I already knew the answer. It was the same reason I'd jumped at the chance to come, despite myself.

"Skip it and day drink?" I asked it as if I could care less either way. At least, I hoped my tone sounded neutral.

For a second, I thought he was going to change his mind. Maybe he really just didn't care either way and was being nice, thinking I didn't feel like skiing.

Shit. My man-reading radar was so fucked up.

Thanks, Makis.

"Sounds good to me. Although I think I'll switch to beer. How about you?"

"I packed a bottle of Tito's, and Pia was supposed to bring club soda."

While Parker looked through the cabinets for a glass, I texted Pia back. She must have been in the lodge because a wink emoji came right back at me. I turned the phone around so Parker wouldn't see it.

"Thanks," I said as he mixed my vodka soda. And just like that, the two of us were in the great room, fire started, also courtesy of Parker, looking out onto the slopes with drinks in hand.

"I could get used to this," he said, sinking into the couch. I was already sitting cross-legged on the loveseat caddy-corner to him.

"No kidding. This place is incredible."

"So are you."

It took a second for his words to penetrate.

My first instinct was to remind him that we were just friends. Thankfully, something held me back. A little voice inside my head that reminded me I was very unlikely never to kiss another guy in my life. That as much as I wanted to stay single, to never get hurt again, that was probably not realistic.

A little voice that found itself forming words which could very likely get me into trouble, the two of us alone in this big house day drinking while the others were skiing.

"Thank you," I said, knowing I should leave it at that. Except, I didn't want to. God help me, I wanted more from him. "I feel the same about you."

14

PARKER

A younger version of me would have already found a reason to join Delaney on the couch an hour ago, when she said, "I feel the same about you."

The thirty-one-year-old version of me was more cautious, for various reasons. But goddamn, if the woman wasn't as incredible as I'd said she was. Before I even had a chance to respond, Delaney bounded off the couch earlier, claiming she needed "to pee." Either the woman had the smallest bladder on the planet or she hadn't really planned to blurt that out. If she regretted saying it or not, I still wasn't sure. But I did know my stomach hurt from laughing.

Delaney was a hoot. Not always from trying. She called them "blonde moments" but I'd told her that was a slander to blondes everywhere, which earned me a pillow to the head. One I had been dearly tempted to pick up and carry over to her to show Delaney what an adult pillow fight looked like. Namely, with her pinned underneath me, the pillow under her head, at the end.

"Another drink?" I asked as the conversation took a decidedly flirty turn. It had started out with Delaney telling me about her "smut books" and me asking for more details and... here we were.

"Sure," she said, standing up with me. "You know we're going to be shitfaced by the time the others get back," she said. "Maybe I should down a water first."

"Or two," I said, knowing one water was not going to make up for what we'd drunk so far. Heading to the cabinet of glasses, I grabbed two and filled them with ice and water. Handing one to Delaney, I leaned against the kitchen counter.

"So back to your smut books."

"How did I know we were going to circle back to that?" she teased.

"We don't have to." I tried to play nice. But she looked so damn sexy, drinking her water, as innocent as can be. Or maybe not so innocent. Delaney tilted her head down and peered up at me through her lashes. She probably didn't even realize she was doing it, but the gesture was flirty.

Sexy.

I couldn't ignore it.

Putting my water down, I headed to where she was standing. As luck would have it, Delaney was right in front of the bottle of Tito's. As I leaned toward her, she didn't move. She did look at my lips, though, and dammit if I didn't want to kiss her so badly it was physically painful. On one hand, she'd been flirty today. Her body language told me to lean in. To kiss her. Pull her hips into mine and feel how well our bodies fit together.

On the other, she had made it clear the other day that we were friends.

Being friendzoned by someone you pictured naked, someone you'd imagined kissing so many times it almost felt as if you knew what they tasted like, was the worst sort of torture.

I reached behind her.

Delaney, realizing my purpose there, so close to her, put her hand on my chest. The feather-light touch should not have made my dick begin to harden, but it did. Resisting the urge to adjust myself, I took a deep breath. Willed it to behave.

Looking into those clear hazel eyes, trying to discern her intent, I waited for another sign. One that told me Delaney had changed her mind about her "this is not a date" talk from lunch.

Her lips parted.

"There's the ski skippers."

One second, I had been about to lean in. The next, I grabbed the bottle of Tito's from behind her and moved back so quickly that I doubted Beck noticed much.

"Back so soon?" I asked as he took off his boots and coat, hanging them near the door.

"We were on the slopes by nine. Someone's legs were tired. Give you one guess who couldn't keep up." He shook out the dirty blond surfer-looking mane more than one woman had lost their mind over.

Instead of answering his question, I made Delaney's drink.

"Pia will probably have one too," she said as Pia and the others filed inside.

"One what?" Mason's fiancée said, taking off her boots and coat too.

"Guess," Beck prompted me again. "Who wanted to quit?"

With a semi-hard dick and thoughts of Delaney's lips parting, I wasn't in the mood for Beck's games.

He grabbed my shoulders from behind.

"You are no fun," he said with a friendly shake.

"Cole," I said, playing along.

"Yep. I think he's getting soft. Tell him to move out of the city and join us." When Beck released my shoulders, I continued to make drinks. Delaney had slid another glass next to hers.

"Cole," I said as he wiped his glasses on his shirt and put them on. "Beck wants you to quit your job, forget about tenure at Columbia, and come live with us at the inn."

Mason snorted. "You are a real piece of work. He has a *job*."

"Oooh, is that for me?" Pia said, spying the drinks I'd made. "Keep one on ice. My ass is frozen... I'm gonna take a super quick shower to warm up."

She headed for the stairs. To no one's surprise, Mason followed her.

"Anyone want a vodka soda?" I asked Cole and Beck. "I have a feeling they're not going to be back anytime soon."

"I'll take it," Beck said. The guy was an indiscriminate alcohol drinker. Scotch. Beer. Vodka. Wine. You name it, he drank it.

Cole made his way over to the liquor counter where there was entirely too much alcohol for one overnighter.

"Nice," I said, spying the bottle of Glenlivet. Knowing Cole, likely a twelve-year-old bottle. "You don't fuck around."

"Depends on what you're referencing."

Only Cole had a way of making a sexual innuendo sound classy.

"Oh, yeah?" Beck asked. "Do tell."

"Grab me one," I said as Beck went for a beer in the fridge.

"I don't kiss and tell, unlike someone I know," Cole said, heading toward the sliding glass doors. "This is one hell of a view."

Beck handed me a beer and joined Cole. "No shit. Nice job scoring the house."

Alone in the kitchen, although still within earshot of the guys, Delaney and I looked at each other. "Cheers," I said, lifting my bottle. At this point, I was feeling pretty good and assumed Delaney was too. Though no sign of a slur. The girl could hold her alcohol.

"So much for water."

"One glass is better than none."

She laughed. "I'm definitely gonna need a break to make it all night."

That gave me an idea. One that would allow us a little more alone time... with other benefits too. "What if we finish these and watch the sunset." I nodded toward the guys. "Then take a drink break in the hot tub?"

She blinked. "A hot tub... break?"

"Sure. I saw one on the deck when we came in."

"Same." She cocked her head to the side, considering. "I did bring my suit, just in case."

"Perfect. What'dya think?"

"We can't completely lose our buzz. I'll be crawling in my bed before we have a chance to play Cards Against Humanity."

"Ahhh, I wasn't aware we were making it a game night?"

"Pia would never miss an opportunity for games. I think she brought like five of them."

"Good thing I like playing games."

"Do you?" Her tone was suggestive.

I looked her dead in the eyes. "Not with people," I said as sincerely as possible. Whether she believed me or not, I couldn't be sure. Delaney had been burned pretty badly, and I wouldn't blame her if she didn't. But I wasn't that kind of guy.

Namely, a narcissistic asshole who only gave a shit about himself and being in control. I knew guys like Makis and I wasn't one of them. Nor would I be friends with someone like that. He could fucking go to hell, and if I ever met the dickhead,

I'd be tempted to send him there myself. Or at least lay him flat on the ground for how he'd treated Delaney.

"Good to know," she said.

"Card games, though? Sure."

Her smile told me that was the right answer. "Good."

I waited.

"Sunset then hot tub break. Let's do it."

I nodded toward the guys just as the sun began dipping below the distant mountains. Before Delaney got to us, I whispered to them both, "You don't want to join us."

"Huh?" Beck asked as Delaney reached us.

"Oh, wow," she said. "I didn't think the view could get any better. That's like a postcard."

I watched her instead of the sunset, but agreed. The view was spectacular.

"We're going to hit the hot tub," she said to Beck and Cole. "If you guys are interested."

Beck cleared his throat.

"Uhhh." Cole looked at me, then to Beck. "I think I'll pass for now. Maybe later tonight."

"Agreed," Beck said. "We have a lot of catching up to do." He raised his beer bottle.

Which, of course, he could do in the hot tub. But still, it was the right answer.

"Suit yourself," she said. "I'll mention it to Pia," Delaney said, "and go change."

"Great. See you in a few."

Neither Beck nor Cole said a word, but their looks weren't exactly subtle. We may have lost Mason to Pia, but the guys clearly didn't relish the idea of another one biting the dust. I raised my bottle in a silent salute to our shared history and followed Delaney up the stairs just as Pia and Mason's door opened.

"I was just going to text Pia," Delaney said to Mason. "Do you guys want to hit the hot tub with us?"

He looked past her, at me. I shook my head.

"Maybe later," he said. "Just took a shower."

"Oh, right," she said, continuing to climb the stairs. "Looks like it's just the two of us," Delaney called down to me.

"Looks like it," I said.

Such a shame.

15

DELANEY

"Ummm..." Pia closed the door behind her, sitting on my bed. "What's happening?"

Apparently she got my "SOS" text.

"I'm going in the hot tub. With Parker."

"Okay," she said, clearly not seeing the problem.

"Alone. Apparently no one else wants to join us."

"Don't look at me like that. I just got out of the shower." Pia cocked her head to the side. "But do you really want company, anyway?"

"No. Yes. I don't know."

"Talk to me."

My head was a jumbled mess. "He's incredible." That wasn't what I'd expected to blurt out, but there it was. "I could talk to him all night. We sort of both agreed to stay back, and after a few drinks... I dunno. If you guys hadn't come home that very second, I think he may have kissed me."

"Is that so bad? You just said he's incredible. Which, I agree. Parker is one of the nicest guys I know."

My heart raced. "I know he's not Makis. But honest to God, I really don't want to go through what I did with him again. A broken heart is no joke."

"Let's think about this. First of all, you haven't even kissed the guy yet. That's a far cry from full-on relationship status. Second, you said yourself, Parker is not Makis. I would never encourage you if he was."

"You think I should go for it?"

"I think you'd be a fool not to. I also know for a fact Parker is more than a little hesitant in the 'getting serious' department too, so in a warped way, you guys are perfect for each other. Just have fun, and live in the moment. Don't worry about the future. You know?"

I nodded. "I do. You're right."

Pia laughed. "That's what they all say."

We stood up. I hadn't brought a robe so I'd wrapped a towel around me. Thankfully I had thought to bring flip-flops. Putting those on and grabbing a hair tie, I said, "Ready."

Pia opened my bedroom door and gave me a final "you got this" look as we headed downstairs.

All three guys were in the kitchen, drinks in hand, and they turned to look at me as I walked toward them, pretending to act casual.

"He's out there already," Cole said, his measured voice almost soothing.

"Thanks." I headed toward one of the sliding glass doors. It was dark now, but a string of white lights across the deck's roof gave off enough light to see easily. I sucked in my breath as a blast of cold hit me when I opened the door. Scurrying to the hot tub and trying not to notice Parker's state of undress, I tossed my towel onto a nearby rack and followed up with a less than graceful climb into the hot tub.

I was immersed by the time I noticed Parker watching me.

I'd brought my favorite bikini, a bright boho-print that looked better with a tan, but was still cute.

Speaking of cute...

Parker's arms rested on the edge of the tub on each side of him. As I'd imagined, he was in great shape. Shoulders, chest, biceps... muscles everywhere, but not overdone. His was a naturally toned look, like a guy might get from chopping wood or something.

"Nice suit," he said, his tone as flirty as it had been in the kitchen earlier.

"Thanks," I said, glad to be warm again. From here, soft lights from inside glowed, highlighting how truly large the house was. "This place is so incredible."

"It is," Parker agreed. "It's making me think about how much I enjoyed the log cabin projects."

"You can't do more of them?"

"If I had my own company, maybe. Even so, they aren't all that common."

He trailed off. Trying not to focus on the fact that Parker had no shirt on, and looked damn good without one, I stayed on a topic that seemed safe. "So what's stopping you from starting your own company? You mentioned it briefly, but there has to be more to it."

He sighed. "A few things, but mostly that my boss wouldn't take it well. Cedar Falls is a small town, and I'm not sure it could support another home builder. I could branch out into other projects, but new homes is what I enjoy most. Having someone come to us with an idea, or inkling, of their future home and then watching the whole project come to fruition. Giving them the keys and seeing the look on a new homeowner's face the first time it all comes together. It's priceless."

"Alright," I said, unable to resist. "They call you 'the nice one' which is clearly accurate. You're funny. Not terrible looking. And now I learn you're a romantic too? What's the catch?"

"Not terrible looking, huh?"

"Not my point."

"I know."

"So what is it? Terrible temper? Stubbornness? Perfectionism?"

"That's quite a list," he said. "Collect those from past experiences?"

"Nah," I said, teasing him. "Those are just a few of my own areas of weakness."

He had the best laugh in the world. "Try again, cupcake."

Cupcake.

It was the silliest nickname ever, but I instantly loved it. "Cupcake?" I said with a smile, telling him as much.

"Yeah, cupcake. Which is my weakness, by the way."

"Cupcakes are your weakness?"

"Yep. Can't stay away from them."

"Stop. You're totally teasing."

"Not teasing," he said.

I gave him a look.

"Fine. One flaw. I have a real fear of commitment. Daddy issues, as they say."

"Is that a flaw, though?"

"Some would say it is."

"Then I guess I have the same flaw."

"So we're just two not-terrible-looking people, afraid of commitment, who like cupcakes."

"How do you know I like cupcakes?"

"Because you smiled when I said it. And also because anyone who doesn't is a real monster, and I typically don't languish in a hot tub with monsters."

Of all Parker's qualities, his silliness was my favorite. "I do like cupcakes," I admitted.

"Of course you do."

For the first time all day, we both went quiet. It wasn't because I didn't have anything to say. There were a million other questions I wanted to ask him. But as I watched Parker look at me the way he did, all of them seemed unimportant.

Except one.

Do you want to kiss me?

It looked like he did. But Parker didn't move. Was it because I'd made it clear we were just friends?

"You know how, at lunch, I made it clear we weren't on a date? And that we were just friends?"

"I do. Very well," he said dryly.

"That was the fear talking."

"What are you afraid of, Delaney?"

Easy question to answer. "Of getting hurt again."

He frowned. "I wish I could promise you never will. Only thing I can say is that I would never willfully hurt you."

I believed him. "I know."

"Do you?"

One second, we sat on opposite ends of the hot tub. The next, he was sitting right beside me. Pushing away a strand of wet hair that had fallen on my cheek, Parker tucked it behind my ear. This was the closest we'd been since the kitchen. I could smell him. Feel him, even though we weren't actually touching.

I looked into his eyes.

"I do," I said, finally answering his question.

Parker's hand moved behind my neck, and he pulled me toward him. Heart hammering, I looked into his kind eyes, which had a glint to them now. A mischievous, sultry, "you are about to be kissed" glint.

I closed my eyes as his lips touched mine. It began slowly, our lips melding together. But when Parker's mouth opened, when his tongue sought my own, the kiss turned quickly. From soft and sensual to something much more urgent. His hand at the back of my neck pulled me closer as the kiss became more insistent. How trite it was to think that this kiss surpassed all others, but honest to God, it was the truth. Our legs pressed together as warm water bubbled around us, the hum of the hot tub the only other sound besides my own murmur of pleasure.

If I could talk to Parker for days, I could kiss him for weeks. Months. Years.

That particular thought had me pulling away. He didn't release the grip on the back of my head, though. Instead, Parker's thumb massaged the soft spot at the top of my spine.

Pure heaven.

"That feels good," I said, meaning it.

He looked directly into my eyes. "Kissing you feels good, Delaney."

The hot tub shut off. Dammit.

"What do you want to do?"

What I wanted to do and what I should do were two different things.

"Should we join the others?" I asked, knowing even as I attempted to preserve my heart that it might be too late. The seal had been broken, so to speak, and I wanted more.

Much more.

"Sure. Don't want the buzz to completely wear off."

"Exactly," I said.

Neither of us moved. I imagined his thumb that continued to rub circles on my neck was somewhere else entirely.

"Keep looking at me like that, cupcake, and we won't be going inside anytime soon."

I smiled, feeling flirty. "And what would you do with me, precisely, if we stayed in here?"

"Hmmm, let's see. I'd probably slip my hand a bit lower and untie that bikini top, for starters. I might fill my hands with those gorgeous breasts of yours, after I moved you to my lap, of course."

Dear lord. You got what you asked for, Delaney.

"I wouldn't have taken you for a dirty talker, Parker. Nice guy and all."

His thumb stopped. Parker's hand moved upward, and before I knew what he was about, it was wrapped around my ponytail. He tugged on it, pulling my head back, lowering his own to my neck. Trailing kisses upward, his teeth nipping ever so slightly, he finished at my ear, my body shivering despite the warmth of the water.

"Looks like you found another of my faults," he whispered. "I do like control."

Holy shit. The pressure of his pull on my hair, combined with his words, was almost too much. And the fact that they came from Parker, someone I'd never predict this side from? My breath caught as his mouth nipped at my ear lobe just before kissing behind it.

I could not breathe. Literally. My chest visibly rose and fell as I attempted to get a hold of myself.

"Overly... controlling?" I squeaked out.

"Just in the bedroom."

"We're in a hot tub," I reminded him.

Parker let go of my hair and shifted just far enough away that our legs were no longer touching. "You're right," he teased, looking around as if just realizing his surroundings. "We are."

I almost said, "A shame."

Because it was. I would very much like to know exactly how

controlling Parker could be, and while I wasn't one to be overly submissive, in any way, we may have just discovered an exception. The idea of him taking control of my mind and body was more than a little appealing.

"Should we go get a drink with the others?"

He stood, Parker's body even more perfect in its entirety than what I'd been able to see so far.

"Sure," I said, making no move to stand just yet. I wasn't sure if I could.

I wasn't sure of anything, actually.

16

PARKER

"And then there was the big love of his life in college," Beck said.

We were hanging around the kitchen island, Delaney sitting next to me on a stool, Pia wrapped in Mason's arms as they leaned against one of the counters, and Cole and Beck sitting on the other stools. Pia tried to get us into the great room, "beautiful roaring fireplace" and all, but not surprisingly, no one wanted to leave the drinks and snacks.

When I'd be in charge of my own home-building business, talking clients into bigger kitchens if they entertained would be a priority.

"Cut me some slack," I warned him, not wanting to scare Delaney away. Especially after that kiss.

"Sophomore year of college, he talked us into this community service project, helping to rebuild homes that were hit hard by an ice storm."

"We weren't easy to convince," Mason added. "Half the time they wanted us on Sundays—"

"Which cut into our recovery time."

"Recovery from what?" Pia asked, looking up at him.

"Partying," Cole said dryly. "Something these guys took seriously in college."

"None of us more so than Beck." Mason took a swig of his beer.

"Anyway." Beck shifted on his stool. "We were working on a house, and an elderly couple lived next door. Mr. Johnson's health wasn't great, and his wife was doing her best to upkeep the house and take care of him."

"She came out whenever we were there," Mason said. "Even made us cookies."

"So of course"—Cole swirled the Scotch in his glass—"one thing led to another, and Parker started doing odd jobs around her house, even after the project was finished."

"Like what?" Delaney asked him.

"Mowing her lawn, fixing a leaky faucet... Things like that."

"She adored him," Mason said.

"I adored her too." I could still see that bright pink lipstick smile clearly in my mind. "She was a retired nurse, so caring for her husband came naturally. Maintaining the house did not."

"If Parker wasn't in class or drinking with us, he was at the Johnsons' house either fixing something or picking up food," Beck said. "We definitely ate better after Parker met his girlfriend."

"Scandalous." Delaney smiled at me. "Since she was already married."

"Unfortunately her husband passed a few months after we first met."

"For almost year"—Beck headed to the fridge and pulled out another beer—"he helped her around the house. Even took her to dinner a few times. Anyone need one?"

"I'll take one," Mason said.

"Unfortunately," I said as Beck handed Mason a beer, "she passed too. Wasn't really even sick, but I think living without him was just too hard. They were married for over sixty years."

"Oh, man," Delaney said. "I'm so sorry."

I took a sip of my drink, knowing if I responded my voice would betray the ache in my chest for a woman who wasn't even related to me but whose death had hit hard. I hadn't lost anyone at that point in my life so had no idea how to cope.

"It's not like you to bring the vibe down," Pia teased Beck.

"Sorry, but Delaney has to know all of Parker's past girlfriends."

He was jumping the gun a bit, but I didn't say that. It was hard to hide the fact that I was into Delaney, and it seemed she reciprocated. "Pretty sure she doesn't," I countered.

"Speaking of the hot tub," Beck said, cheeky as ever, "how was it? I'm thinking it's time to check it out."

"Great," Delaney said. "I mean..." She tried not to smile. "It was fine."

"Fine, huh?" I asked, wanting to say more but also not wanting to embarrass her.

"Good enough for me. Who's in?"

"Shit." Everyone looked at Cole, who was staring at his phone.

"What's up?" I asked.

"Apparently we're getting some snow now tomorrow. No idea where that came from."

"How long have you lived up here?" Mason asked. Since he'd grown up with Cole in Cedar Falls, it was a rhetorical question that Mason knew the answer to already.

"Snow storms and upstate New York are pretty much a

thing," Beck added, just in case Cole didn't already know that. I smiled at the look Cole gave him, as if Beck was a wayward child and Cole was his father. Usually after a few drinks he was warmed up pretty good and let loose a bit, but uptight Cole returned pretty quickly.

I snuck a glance at Delaney next to me. She'd changed out of her bathing suit into leggings and a sweatshirt. Hair in a messy bun, the casual look suited her. Very well, actually.

She caught me staring. Delaney's thick lashes framed the most beautiful big eyes that had begun to soften toward me, and the corners of her lips turned up ever so slightly. A half smile that was part pleasure, part allure. It was as if she was remembering that kiss. Not that I blamed her. Who could forget it?

Coming back to the conversation, I picked up that a storm was coming late morning tomorrow. Cole worried about getting back to the city in time for a Tuesday-morning class since the snow was apparently going to last all day.

"I'm already off tomorrow," I said. "You head out in the morning. At least I'll know what I'm talking about with the roofing guys."

"You sure?" Cole asked.

"Positive." I gestured to the house. "Forced to stay here another night? It's not much of a hardship, trust me."

Cole turned to Mason and Pia. "You guys okay with heading out on the earlier side? I'll drop you off at the inn and hit the road from there."

"This is why you need to move back," Beck said, relentless in his pursuit to have all four of us together, as if staying at the inn was a permanent thing. Eventually Mason and Pia would get married, the inn's updates would be complete, and there would be no good reason to stay.

"Be serious," Cole said.

"Why?" Beck asked.

"It's no problem," Pia interjected. "We can be up and Adam whatever time you want."

"Up and Adam?" Mason asked. "Who says that?"

"I do," she insisted.

"That alright with you?" Cole asked Delaney.

She looked at me.

It was her slight hesitation that told me to go for it. "Not sure what time you work on Tuesday, but maybe we can even get in our ski day after I meet with the roofer. Maybe crash another night and head out Tuesday morning."

"Actually," she said, "I'm closing Tuesday and don't go in until one."

"Perfect, but it's up to you."

Every single person in the kitchen turned to poor Delaney.

"You don't have to decide right this second," I said, letting her off the hook. "Let me know."

"Whelp," Beck said, heading toward the fridge. "I for one am making use of the hot tub." He took out a beer. "Come on, party pooper," he said to Cole. "Refill your drink and get the hell out there."

Cole rolled his eyes. "It's like dealing with a fifteen-year-old," he said to no one in particular.

"And you're like dealing with an eighty-year-old. Let's go."

The two of them headed upstairs to change, leaving the four of us in the kitchen.

"Gotta pee. Be right back," Pia said to Mason.

I turned to Delaney. Hopeful, but knowing that a kiss was one thing, an overnight alone... completely another.

"You sure you don't mind some company tomorrow night?" she asked.

In response, I got off the stool, took her glass as if to refill her drink but used the opportunity to whisper into her ear so that Mason couldn't hear me.

"Just the opposite, cupcake. I'm very much looking forward to it."

17

DELANEY

"Do you miss being a cop?"

Mason and Pia sat on the big couch. Parker was on the smaller one, and when I'd come back from the bathroom and the three of them had moved to sit in front of the fire, I panicked. The armchair was cozy, especially since I was closest to the fire. But I should have been brave enough to sit by Parker.

My mind was a jumbled mess of contradictions. Wanting to kiss him again. Wanting to get in the first car out of here tomorrow, go home, and bury myself in my bed. Wanting to bury myself in Parker's bed. Wanting to go back in time and not have kissed him at all.

How could a person want so many opposite things at once?

Makis. That's how.

A huge part of me wanted to forget the sleepless nights I spent waiting for a text that never came. Or the emptiness of life without a man who clearly wasn't right for me but who I missed nonetheless. But the hurt was still there, lingering.

Maybe it was good we weren't sitting together. He looked so handsome in sweats. Though his hair was dry, when it had been wet earlier, it was all I could do to stop myself from running my hands through it.

Mason had just taken a swig of beer when I asked the question.

"Yes and no," he said. "I miss my colleagues and certain aspects of the job. Helping people, which is why I got into it in the first place. But there's a lot of bullshit I don't miss. And running Heritage Hill has been rewarding too." He looked at Pia.

She was lying on the couch with her feet in his lap. Winking at him, Pia snuggled down into the couch even more.

"It must have been scary though? Changing careers like that?"

"It was until I actually made the decision. After that"—he shrugged—"no looking back."

"Which begs the age-old question," Parker said. "What would you do if fear wasn't holding you back?"

I nearly spit out my drink.

"You" didn't seem like an appropriate answer.

"I'd make art my career," I answered quickly, before my cheeks turned pink and everyone guessed what had really been on my mind.

"You should see her paintings," Pia said. "There are a few around town actually. The Grapevine Bistro has two, and we've commissioned a big one for the inn's great room."

"Speaking of that," I added. "It'll probably be next month before it's finished."

"No problem," Pia said. "She won't even let me peek," she told Mason.

"You make jewelry too, right?" Parker asked.

"I do. And pottery. That's part of the problem. I can't seem to choose one medium, so am half good at all of them."

"Not true." Pia turned on her side. "She's just being humble."

"Agreed," Mason chimed in. "I've seen your piece at The Big Easy. It's amazing."

"Maggie was so sweet to work with," I said of The Big Easy's chef and owner. "I loved that painting. The subject made it easy to create."

"New Orleans?" Parker asked.

"Yep. She wanted to capture the architecture of the Quarter so I drew a street lined with Creole townhouses."

"Wait a minute," he said. "The picture hanging just behind the hostess stand with all of the colorful houses. That's yours?"

"Yep," Pia chimed in, as if she were my agent or PR rep. "Sure is. Looks like a photo, it's so realistic. Right?"

"Impressive." Parker looked at me. "What's the biggest hurdle?"

"Where do I even start? Giving up guaranteed income. Throwing away years of education. Startup costs. I'd open a studio. Something that could showcase all of my own pieces but a place where other people could learn too and take classes. Somewhere near the square."

"I think she should do it," Pia said.

"Seems like the two of you have a lot in common." Mason got up from the couch to add a log to the fire. "Parker has been talking about his own construction company for years."

Parker and I exchanged a glance. "You're in a better position than me," I said. "Already working in construction. I totally think you should do it."

"I will if you do," he teased, smiling.

"Would love to see that." Mason moved Pia's feet off him. "Who's up for midnight pizza?"

"Me, please," Pia said, looking more awake than she was a few seconds ago. "I'll help."

Whether Mason really needed help putting a frozen pizza in the oven or she wanted to leave Parker and me alone, I'd have to wait to find out.

"So," I said, attempting to keep my tone light. "We both have commitment issues. Both want to start our own companies. Both like cupcakes. What else do we have in common?"

Parker leaned forward, elbows on his knees as if ready for an intense conversation. "Let's find out. Chocolate or vanilla?"

"Chocolate."

He shook his head. "Nope, vanilla. Beach or mountain?"

"Beach."

"Zero for two. Mountains for me. Favorite season?"

"Fall. One hundred percent."

"Oh, man, we're not doing so great. I'm a summer guy. Fishing. Boating. But fall isn't so bad."

"Morning person or night owl?" I asked.

"Morning, for sure."

I grimaced. "You're right. We're sucking it up. How about dream destination?"

Parker raised his eyes, looking straight up toward the bedrooms upstairs. "Pleading the fifth on that one. Mace, grab me a beer?"

I laughed, ignoring the rush of heat that coursed through me at his insinuation. I had to admit, my bedroom with him in it... or his bedroom with me in it... sounded pretty dreamy to me. "I meant for a vacation, silly."

"Oh, well, in that case, Montana. Let me guess from the look on your face, not your top pick?"

Funny he'd say Montana. "No," I said. "That would be Italy. I've always wanted to see it."

We talked about the places we had been and tried to find more commonalities until Mason and Pia finished cooking. By then, the other guys came back inside from the hot tub, changed, and joined what turned out to be our late-night pizza party.

It was all fun and games until everyone started going to bed. Alone with Parker once again, reluctant to leave him, I asked if he was tired.

"Not even a little. You?"

"Nope," I said, glad to go back to sharing favorites, trying to find more things in common. Having stopped drinking, I was content to talk to Parker and listen to the crackle of the fireplace. I hadn't looked at my phone in a while, but the last time I did peek, it was past three in the morning. Fighting sleep, I stayed awake as Parker headed into the bathroom, wondering if I should get up and join him on the couch. Maybe I would, but only after I closed my eyes for a second. Just a tiny little nap until he came back.

18

PARKER

Coffee in hand, I wandered over to the sliding glass doors. The sun wasn't up yet, nor were any of my housemates. Delaney must have gotten up at some point during the night after she'd fallen asleep. The blanket that I'd put on top of her after she dozed off was still on the couch, but it was otherwise empty.

Pia assured me that Delaney had the ability to fall asleep on a dime, and that I shouldn't take it personally. After how much we'd drunk, and lulled by the warmth of the fire at three in the morning, it hadn't even occurred to me to do so, but Pia's reassurance was welcome anyway. She and Delaney were close, and the fact that Pia worried at all about my reaction told me something about Delaney's state of mind.

I took a sip of coffee just as the sun began to peek over the mountain.

What a spectacular view. When I built my own house, I'd be sure to position it similarly. Watching the sun rise always gave me a sense of peace and hope for the day. It was part of the reason I enjoyed fishing so much, being up and out early enough to watch the world come awake.

Delaney.

As I watched the sunrise, I thought of my last glimpse of her, fast asleep on the couch. With luck, I'd never run into her asshole ex. The last time I'd gotten into a fight was in college, and I'd prefer to keep it that way, but there was no chance I would be able to keep myself from punching that dickhead in the face if I ever met him. I didn't blame him for breaking up with her but for messing with her head. Clearly he'd done a number on her. Controlling piece of shit.

It was probably good she fell asleep. After that kiss, I'd wanted to scoop Delaney up and set her on my lap as we talked. In that position, there was very little chance we'd have only talked, either. Kissing her had been the highlight of my week.

Month.

Year.

"You slept in," I said as Mason joined me.

"It's a hell of a lot harder to wake up at the crack of dawn with a woman like Pia by your side."

"I bet."

"Speaking of Pia and her friends..."

"Were we though?"

"She's been through hell, Park. Pia worries about her."

"I can tell." I turned toward my friend. "Did you meet him?"

"Makis? Yeah, once. He's as much of a douchebag as you'd think. But a charmer. She's way too good for him."

"Obviously." I turned toward my friend. "I like her."

"I figured you would. It's hard to believe the two of you never met before now."

"From what I understand, she wasn't in town a lot."

"True. But still."

I caught his eye. I might not have grown up with him like Cole and Beck, but the four of us were inseparable since freshman year of college. I knew him pretty well, and Mason was worried.

"What?"

Mason took a deep breath, let it out and stared me down. "You're the only one I'd let date my sister."

"You don't have a sister."

"But if I did."

"What about Cole?" Beck, I got. But Cole was just about perfect. Smart. Successful. Cultured.

"He's a fucking sexual deviant."

I laughed. "That's stretching it, I think." The four of us didn't go into detail about our sex lives, but we knew enough. He liked things kinkier than the average guy.

"Maybe, but if I did have a sister, I wouldn't want to imagine her—"

"I'll pass on those details," I said. "Your point?"

"My point is, Pia cares about Delaney. A lot. She was the first person who befriended her when Pia came to Cedar Falls. Just... keep that in mind."

"Seriously?" Mason should know me better than that. I wasn't the sort of guy to screw someone over. Not Pia's friend, or any woman.

"You took the pact for a reason," he reminded me. "I think you agreed to it because you didn't want to end up like your father. Delaney's been through the wringer already. That's all I'm saying."

"I'm well aware." I took a sip of coffee, trying not to be offended by Mason's words. He was just looking out for Pia's friend. And was right. "I'm not promising anything I can't deliver on. We're just getting to know each other."

"Never stay the night." Cole. Also an early riser, but not usually this early. "Good coffee, Park."

"Thanks," I said as he joined us. "I'm not sure the rule classifies."

"Certainly does," he said. "You two will be staying here. Alone. Fits the definition to me."

"Except, we're not dating," I argued, well aware Cole was trying to weasel his way into me putting more money in the pot. We'd each chipped in two hundred and fifty bucks when we came up with the pact and its "rules," agreeing to a hundred dollars if we broke one and five hundred for the biggie... marriage.

You took the pact for a reason.

A good reason. Despite the fact that Mason had succumbed, the truth was... the pact had been a good idea. A reminder to remember how things ended when clouded by the euphoria of how things began. I shook away the thought. For now.

"We didn't differentiate," Mason said. "You don't stay the night because of where it leads. Simple. I tossed it in the first time I stayed with Pia."

"I've contributed a few hundred myself," Cole said.

"Right. Same here. But that was different," I argued. "We're not together. Delaney and I are only staying because of the storm."

"Sure, and I'm Peter Pan," Cole said. "You two are Lost Boys, and we're not really at Crystal Peak but Neverland."

"Does that make Pia a mermaid? Or Tinkerbell?" Mason asked. "She looks more like a mermaid to me."

"Who looks like a mermaid?" Pia asked from the kitchen. Mason didn't seem surprised she was behind us. He was always aware of everything, even if it didn't show. As he often said, once a Ranger, always a Ranger. That plus his experience in the NYPD made him impossible to sneak up on.

"You. Long story," he said as she poured herself a coffee.

"I bet. Cole, what time do you want to head out?"

"Sooner the better. I might as well go up and drag Beck's ass out of bed now. If we wait for him to get up we'll be snowed in."

Beck typically kept bartender hours, which meant he wouldn't be up on his own for a few more hours.

"Alright," Pia said. "One coffee, with this view, and I'll get ready to go."

Within the hour, all four of them were packed and getting ready to hit the road when Delaney made her way downstairs. She wore black leggings and a sweatshirt, hair in a ponytail. She didn't have makeup on that I could see, but Delaney didn't need any. Perfectly arched brows and pink cheeks, she was sexy and cute all wrapped in one fine package.

"Good morning, sleeping beauty," Pia said, smiling.

"How long have you all been up?"

"Not long," Beck said. "Cole wanted to hit the road early. It's already starting to flurry."

"Last chance to escape me," I said to lighten the mood. The two of us had been staring at one another for long enough to be noticed.

"You don't think we'll have a problem getting out tomorrow?" she asked.

"Nah. Not with the truck."

"Alright. Then I'm going back to bed," she teased. "With some coffee."

With some final packing up and after a round of goodbyes, Pia and the guys headed out. Seconds ago, the house was full of voices, but now... just the two of us.

"You really going back to bed?"

"Nah," Delaney said. "Although it's tempting. You should see the view from my bedroom."

I'd like to.

Keeping that thought to myself, I asked if she wanted break-fast. "They left most of the food. Bagel?"

"Sure."

A knock at the door interrupted us. The roofing guy.

"I'll grab the bagel myself," Delaney said. "Are you still inter-ested in hitting the slopes when you're done?"

"Absolutely," I said. "After staring at them all morning, I'm ready to get out there."

"Alright. I'll get ready so we can leave as soon as you're done."

"Sounds good."

Walking to the door, I watched Delaney climb the stairs, glad for the roofer. I needed a distraction from the fact that she would be, in a few minutes, up there taking off her clothes.

Never stay the night.

We'd debated our "bachelor pact" rules for days, eventually coming up with that one, agreeing that an overnighter brought things to another level. Mason might have been right to caution me. There was something about her that told me this particular overnighter would do just that.

I wanted her.

Craved another kiss.

Craved having her in my arms. In my bed.

More importantly, though, I liked her. A lot.

You took that pact for a reason.

And that was the scariest thought of them all.

19

DELANEY

I suspected he was going to kiss me on the way out of the house when we all but bumped into each other. And then again, in the car on the short ride to the slopes. Parker looked over at me so intently as he pulled into the parking spot, I was certain of it.

Instead, he got out and proceeded to put on his ski boots.

I hadn't skied in years, and actually never had my own equipment, so after tickets and rentals, we headed to the slopes.

"I don't mind if you want to hit the bigger hills. It's all green for me," I said as we made our way to the lift.

Parker fit in perfectly here. By the way he moved, it was clear he was a good skier. Probably a natural athlete, one of those guys who was good at everything.

"No way," he said. "I'm with you."

It sounded so... comforting... the way he said it. Like the warm blanket he'd laid over me last night. I'd nearly melted when I realized what he'd done.

Never mind that I woke up in the middle of the night to an empty room, the guy I thought maybe, possibly, I'd end up with nowhere to be seen. But instead of being embarrassed this morning that I'd conked out, Parker made me feel immediately at home.

Like now.

"I guess it's like a bicycle," I said, skiing toward the lift. "I haven't done this in years."

"Once a skier, always a skier," he said as we waited in line. Since it was Monday, and with the storm, the place was all but abandoned. It was a short line with only four people ahead of us. We boarded quickly and headed up the mountain.

"Sorry for falling asleep on you last night," I said as we made our way up. The flurries were getting heavier, making the ski resort look like a postcard.

"There's nothing to be sorry for. We put in a shift and a half of drinking."

"And didn't even use the Baileys for hot tub cocoa."

"There's always tonight."

We were close enough that our legs were touching, not that I could feel anything with our ski pants between us. I turned to him, thinking about drinking spiked hot chocolate in the hot tub later. "That sounds good," I said, having given this whole situation a lot of thought this morning.

I could either live in the past and worry about the future or embrace the present. Take things as they come and try not to get inside my head too much. Carpe diem and all that. Which is exactly what I planned to do.

"Sounds better than good to me."

We were nearly halfway up. Just enough time to...

Parker leaned into me. Closing my eyes, breathing in the cold, crisp air, I met him halfway. His lips were soft and warm, like a sip of that hot cocoa we'd talked about, making my insides all melty. Our tongues met, and we immediately picked up where we left off last night. I could have kissed him for hours, but thankfully one of us realized we were still on a ski lift. He pulled back just in time.

The lift operator must have seen couples like us all the time. He didn't even blink as we scrambled to ski off. Thankfully, even between being rusty on skis and that kiss, I was able to stay on my feet.

"Green Valley work for you?"

"Sure," I said, following him to what I knew was one of the gentlest slopes. My father taught me to ski here, and it was the first one I'd ever skied on my own.

"Race to the bottom?" he asked as we slowed at the top of the hill. "Kidding," he said, before I could respond. "Just take it nice and slow. There's hardly anyone here."

I was just about to push off when he added, "You've got this, cupcake."

Jamming my poles into the ground, I stopped. Looked at him. And nearly said something I probably would have regretted. Instead I simply smiled and said, "Thanks. I'm ready."

Parker stayed with me the entire time, and like down below on the flat surface, it really did come back quickly. By the time we got to the bottom third, I was already letting myself pick up speed.

You've got this, cupcake.

I nearly blurted, "I love when you call me that," but, thankfully, I caught the words before they came out of my mouth. It was one lesson my mother had tried to instill, to think before I talked, that I never quite followed. She said it made me appear flightier than I really was, but I never really agreed with her. Being honest, saying what was on my mind, was just... me. For better or worse.

"See?" he asked as I immediately skied back to the short lift line.

"You were right," I said as the couple in front of us boarded.

Just like that, we were on our way up again. This time, Parker didn't wait. As soon as the safety bar was down, he leaned into me. This kiss was not at all like the last one. His mouth opened immediately, Parker and I melding together as if we would consume each other.

"If I've ever tasted anything sweeter in my life," he said, pulling back, "I can't remember it."

"Stop," I said, swatting him. "That's such a line."

"No," he said, serious. "It's not. Although I'm pretty certain if your lips taste that good, there is one thing that will taste even better."

Before the shock of his words could register—Parker was the "nice" one, after all—it was time to dismount. I'd have talked to Parker about what he said, except the devilish man skied right over to the run. With a quick look back to ensure I was there, presumably, he was off. This time, I did race him. My ski legs were back, much more quickly than I had anticipated.

And so it went.

Lift after lift. After the fourth kiss when Parker asked, "Where do you like to be kissed most?" just as we dismounted, I decided to take him to task on the next run. We'd graduated to one of the steeper green runs, and I thought a challenge might be fun. So when he pulled the bar down, I said, "You obviously like bets, the whole bachelor thing and all."

"That's more of a pact than a bet," he said.

"Maybe a little of both?"

"Maybe," he conceded. "What are you thinking?"

"If I try an intermediate run"—Parker's eyes widened—"you have to say the dirtiest thing you can think of on our next lift."

"Excuse me?"

"You heard me," I teased. Flirting with him had become my new favorite pastime. "Obviously you're a bit of a dirty talker."

He tried not to smile. "Noticed that, huh?"

"Uh. Yeah."

"Does it bother you?"

Was he serious? "No, just the opposite," I admitted.

"Good." He leaned over for a quick kiss since we were more than halfway up the hill.

Scratch that. Kissing Parker was my new favorite pastime.

"So, is it on?" I asked.

"Like Donkey Kong."

Laughing, I nearly stumbled dismounting, but Parker caught me. I couldn't really feel his hand through the glove and snow jacket, but the fact that he was touching me did something to my insides. Like his kisses, it was as if the cold couldn't get to me. Usually by now I'd have been begging to go into the lodge to warm up, but with Parker by my side, I wanted to ride this lift all day.

"Whispering Pines?"

"Sure," I said. "Wait, does it have moguls?"

"Nope."

Sure enough, I was worried for nothing. Parker stayed with me the entire time, but Whispering Pines wasn't all that much more challenging than the hardest beginner run.

When we got to the bottom, though, there was something about Parker's expression that gave me pause.

"What is it?" I asked, certain he was up to something.

"Hate to say it, cupcake, but I have to hit the little boy's room. Quick break in the lodge?"

"Oh, you stinker. Way to get out of your end of the bet."

"Not at all," he said as we skied toward the lodge. "We're not done skiing yet."

And so it was, for the first time in my life, I was less looking forward to sitting by the fire inside the lodge, drink in hand, than I was getting back on that lift and hearing what Parker had to say.

It wasn't until our coats and hats were off and Parker and I cozied up to the bar in the adult section of the lodge, not too far from the fire, that I realized something.

I hadn't thought of the hurt Makis had doled out to me all morning. My chest hadn't felt heavy. My thoughts were not jumbled with confusion. It had simply been a pleasurable— more than pleasurable—day so far.

And best yet?

It wasn't over.

20

PARKER

It was just lunch.

Sandwiches. Homemade chips. Drinks.

There was nothing remarkable about the lodge bar, or the meal. Except...

I couldn't remember a day like this one. A meal like this one. Ever.

Sure, my senses were heightened after that last run. Kissing Delaney, knowing she was as into me as I was her. Of course it would be a rush; the unparalleled excitement of getting to know someone for the first time always was. But not quite like this.

I hadn't lived thirty-one years without being able to sense a difference between other women and the one that was currently putting on her hat beside me. We talked about our families, comparing notes about brothers and sharing the kinds of things people do when they are learning about each other.

I managed to keep my hands off her the entire meal; not because I didn't want to touch her. The exact opposite, actually. I wanted to hold her hand, kiss those soft, full lips, so damn much that Delaney might think it was all I cared about.

Did I want to be with her?

Yes. So fucking much it was almost painful.

But I wanted to get to know her more.

"You look so serious all of a sudden," she said as we geared back up for a few more runs. Agreeing to head back soon with the snow coming down pretty good now, and that beautiful house just waiting for two people to make use of it, we headed back out toward the lift.

The dirtiest thing I can think of.

Obviously, I couldn't exactly say *that* to her. Even though Delaney asked for it, we weren't a couple. Had never done anything more than kiss yet.

"Just making sure you remembered our bet," she said as we skied down toward the lift. With the snow really coming down, the mountain was all but empty. Some diehards remained, scattered around the lodge with a few dotting the ski hills here and there.

"I remember," I said, wishing it was the only bet on the table. The other one, with the guys, was never far from my mind.

We boarded the chair. I pulled down the safety bar. Then, leaning over into Delaney's ear, I lifted up her hat.

Tucked strands of hair behind her ear before I kissed it, gently.

"When I finally get you in my bed, cupcake, which I will... only after you beg me for it... I am going to spread your thighs so wide, I won't even need to use my fingers to open your pussy for me. But I'll use them anyway, my thumbs gently folding you back until my ultimate prize is revealed. I'll use my tongue to make you call my name so loud the neighbors can hear. When you come, I will lick every last fucking drop until you are so spent that you can't even lift your head from the damn pillow."

I pulled her hat down in place. Kissed her nose.

Winked at her and then lifted the safety bar. One step ahead of her, I helped Delaney ski off. As I suspected, or at least hoped, she was a little wobbly coming off the lift.

"You good?" I asked, letting go of her waist and adjusting my poles.

"Honestly? No." She did the same, Delaney skiing to my side. "I wasn't expecting that."

"You did ask for dirty," I said. "Of course, if that's not something you're into—"

"Are you kidding me right now? What woman isn't into... that?"

"This ski trip definitely took a turn." I grinned. "And I like it."

"You and me both," she said, taking off toward the intermediate hills.

We made it two more runs.

By the time Delaney and I got into the truck to head back, I was half tempted not to wait. If it hadn't been the middle of the day, I might not have, but public sex was Cole's thing, not mine.

"I can honestly say"—Delaney turned up the heat on her side—"that was the most enjoyable ski trip of my life."

"Same," I said, wishing we could be transported back to the house. Thankfully, it was a short ride.

"Not that I want you to drive faster in the snow but..." Delaney said when we were just a few minutes away.

I looked at her, thinking the same thing.

"I really, really... have to pee."

Laughing, I stepped on the gas. "That's not what I thought you were going to say."

"No? What were you thinking?"

I turned onto the road that would take us to the house.

"I was thinking you were impatient to get into the house so you could tear my clothes off."

"Did you now?"

When I pulled into the driveway, Delaney didn't waste a second. Before we were barely parked she was halfway up the stairs. Laughing, I closed the truck door and followed. There were a few inches on the ground already, and it was snowing hard. It was a good thing Cole took off when he did.

Moving Delaney's boots to the side, I took off my own, hung up my ski jacket and noticed the bathroom door just off the kitchen was closed. She must be inside.

"Delaney," I called in. "I'm heading up to change my pants. Will be right back down."

"OK," she called back.

Putting on a dry pair of sweats and socks, I headed back downstairs.

No Delaney.

Figuring she must have gone up to change herself, I went to work. Started a fire. Poured wine. At lunch she'd confessed to being in a "red wine mood," and though it wasn't my go-to drink, I didn't mind it either. The others had left the food and drinks when I assured them it wasn't a problem for us to pack up. Pia had brought enough red wine for a week, so by the time Delaney came back downstairs—this time in matching peach sweats and a cropped sweatshirt, hair up in a messy bun—her wine was waiting on the kitchen counter.

"Is this some kind of dream?" she asked, approaching. "The snow." She gestured outside where it was coming down hard now. "A fire. Wine."

Before she could take a glass, I grabbed her hand and pulled her toward me.

"You forgot one thing," I said. It was the first time our bodies were flush against each other. Reaching behind her neck to pull Delaney closer, I groaned with the sheer pleasure of having her so close.

"What's that?" she asked, her arms wrapping around my waist.

"Me," I said, just before claiming her mouth. Immediately opening for me, Delaney gave herself completely to the kiss.

Her breasts pressed against my chest as I pulled her closer. Her fingers gripped the back of my sweatshirt as I broke the kiss to taste more. Her neck, behind her ear, down to her collarbone and lower. I would have lifted her sweatshirt off and kept going if she hadn't jumped.

I pulled away.

"What's wrong?"

She pulled her phone from her pocket. "It scared the shit out of me. I have no idea why the ringer is on. Must have bumped it skiing or something."

Delaney's lips were fuller than usual, swollen from our kiss. Her cheeks flushed, she looked both adorable and hot as fuck.

As always.

I stepped back, already regretting the words I was about to say.

"As much as I would absolutely love to ravish you," I said, reaching for her glass, "maybe we should have a drink. Enjoy the view while it's still light out."

I handed Delaney her wine and took my own.

"Why, Parker Scott," she said in a not so good Southern accent, "are you getting shy on me?"

"Miss Delaney Thorton," I answered with an accent of my own. She laughed. Mine was even worse than hers. "I don't get shy," I said. "If you'd like me to carry you upstairs right now and fuck you until sundown, just say the word."

Delaney's free hand flew to her mouth. "Oh, my. The language on you. And here I thought you were a perfect gentleman," she said, her accent mildly improving.

"Oh, I'm a gentleman alright. But not between the sheets, darlin'."

Her lashes fluttered, Delaney a model of decorum.

Sort of.

"Whatever do you mean, Mr. Scott?"

"I'll gladly show you," I said. "After drinks. And dinner. And another round of the hot tub."

Her bottom lip extended into a perfect pout. "That does seem like such a long time from now."

Smiling, I raised my glass. "The anticipation of pleasure is often better than pleasure itself."

She clinked glasses with me, and we both took a sip of wine.

"Wise words," Delaney said, her fake accent fully intact. "I do hope they're true."

"Not mine. Shakespeare's. And I mean to prove to you later this evening that they are very, very true."

"Quoting Shakespeare? You are just full of surprises, Parker Scott."

"I'm just gettin' started, cupcake."

21

DELANEY

I couldn't take it anymore.

Doubling down on the whole anticipation theme, Parker didn't so much as touch me as we shared a glass of wine in front of the fire, watching as snow continued to fall outside. When we shared leftovers for dinner with no hope of ordering out in this storm, he answered all of my questions. Asked some of his own. But was, unfortunately, the perfect gentleman.

At one point I considered making the first move myself, but it became almost a test of wills. I could restrain myself as well as the next guy. Parker being the next guy in this particular situation.

But enough was enough.

"What do you think?" I asked him as we cleaned up the kitchen. "Time for that spiked hot cocoa now that the sun is down?" Before he could answer, I bolted from the kitchen and up the stairs, calling down, "Last one in their suit is a rotten egg."

Nothing like a bikini to push the balance of power a bit.

Changing into my suit, I took a peek in the full-length

mirror. As much as I wanted to cover up with a towel, that didn't jive with my goal of getting Parker to make good on his chair lift promises. Instead, I grabbed a towel and carried it out of the bedroom with me.

His bedroom door was closed across the hall. Peeking over the balcony and not seeing Parker downstairs, certain he was inside, I walked to the door and lifted my fist to knock. At that exact moment, his door opened.

Standing in front of me with nothing on but his bathing suit, Parker also carrying a towel, whatever I'd planned on saying to him fled straight out of my head. He looked me up and down, as I'd just done to him.

Remembering the sweet torture of the past few hours he'd put me through, I decided a taste of his own medicine was in order. Spinning from him, making sure to give Parker an unobstructed view of my backside, I hurried away and smiled to myself, hearing Parker's mumbled epithet.

"Hot chocolate and Baileys?" I asked, pulling two coffee mugs from the kitchen cupboard.

"Something tells me I'm being punished," Parker said as he emerged from the stairwell into the kitchen. I'd lit a candle on the center of the island, and with just a few lamps and the fireplace for light, the place was even more romantic now than it had been with a view of the storm.

"Maybe a little," I admitted as I made our hot chocolates. "I think I want a ski chalet. I'll admit that was never on my bucket list, but this place just has such a vibe."

"A multi-million-dollar log cabin with a clear view of Crystal Peak? I'd say that's probably on most people's bucket list, skier or not."

"Would you rather this view or the one at Heritage Hill? Of the lake?"

Finished with our drinks, I turned to catch Parker staring at my ass.

"Can I suggest a third option?" he said as I handed him a mug.

"No." I laughed. "Has to be one of those two."

He made another sound, and maybe, just maybe, Parker was regretting his "anticipation of pleasure is often as good as the pleasure itself" stance.

"I'd choose the lake."

With what I was sure was the biggest smile on my face, I grabbed a towel with my free hand and made my way outside, immediately regretting not having wrapped it around me first. It was freezing, but thankfully the porch roof kept most of the snow away. Stepping through stray flakes, I made it to the hot tub.

It was only after we both scrambled into the tub that I realized it had magically uncovered itself. "When did you take the cover off?"

"When you were in the bathroom, just before you suggested coming outside," he said, taking a sip of spiked cocoa.

I did the same, watching how falling snow was reflected in the white bulb lights. So pretty. And then I looked at my companion.

An even better view than the snow.

His bicep muscles flexed as Parker raised the mug to his lips.

"You had the same idea as me?" I asked.

"Ripping off your bathing suit and having my way with you?"

"No," I teased. "Coming out here."

"I did," he said. "Great minds and all that."

I tilted my head to the side. "We really do have a lot in common."

"Tell me what else you like to do in your spare time." He took another sip. "Besides your art."

"I like to read. And hang out with my friends. Eat Mom's homemade meatloaf. Girls' trips. Drink wine and vodka sodas. Hit the gym. Stuff like that."

"Any outdoor activities?"

I thought about that one. "I did have a good time skiing today. I can't believe I went on two intermediates."

"I can. You're a natural."

"Thanks," I said.

"How's your cocoa?"

"Delish. Almost gone though."

"Good."

One second, I had a coffee mug in my hand. The next, it was gone. Parker put both of our mugs on the top of the tub's flat surface and, on his way back into the hot tub, reached for me.

"I didn't have straddling you in the hot tub on my bingo card when I decided to come on this trip," I said.

Wrapping my arms around Parker's neck, I adjusted my legs, finding it a surprisingly comfortable position. And one that told me exactly how much Parker wanted this as much as me.

"No?" He reached around my back, pulling me closer. "I did."

With that, Parker kissed me.

Finally.

And it wasn't just any kiss but one that consumed me, entirely. Our lips melded together, tongues both insistent, as Parker pulled me even closer. Not surprised to feel the straps of my bikini come undone and my bare breasts surrounded by water, I grasped at Parker's hair just as he pulled back.

"I want to see that pretty face," he said, Parker's thumbs

rubbing over my nipples. "When I make these hard beneath my fingers."

"You are a dirty boy, Mr. Parker Scott."

"And I'm gonna get a hell of a lot dirtier," he said, playing with me. I pushed against his hands, wanting to feel them cover me.

Parker complied.

"Tell me," I said, liking the verbal foreplay more than I could have imagined. Who would have thunk it? Nice Parker, a dirty boy.

"The second this hot tub turns off, I am going to lift you out of here, carry you to my bedroom and dry you off. I'll make sure to save your sweet pussy for last so I can spend some extra time there. And then I'm going to make you come first with my fingers, second with my tongue and a third time—"

The hot tub shut off.

Making good on his words, Parker lifted me to standing. He was out of the hot tub, towel around his waist, before I could hardly register what was happening.

"Time to go, cupcake," he said, standing on the platform and holding out his hand.

I took it.

Before I could climb all the way out, he picked me up as if I weighed as much as one of the errant snowflakes that had made its way into the hot tub. Grabbing my towel, he handed it to me and carried me—literally carried me—into the house.

"I thought it was a figure of speech," I said as Parker made his way inside. "I'm not a bride, you know," I teased.

And for the briefest of seconds, I imagined what that would be like. Parker's bride.

Geez Louise, slow down there, Delaney.

"Oh, I know exactly what you are," Parker said as he climbed the stairs. Shivering, I pulled the towel up over my shoulders.

"Do tell," I said, unable to look away. His eyes were usually warm, but right now, they blazed with need. The fact that I did that to him made me want this even more. As if such a thing were possible.

"You are"—he pushed his bedroom door open with his foot —"smart. Funny. Bubbly. Creative. Sexy as hell."

He put me down and immediately grabbed the towel to dry me. "And mine tonight."

Parker didn't seem to be cold despite the fact that he was still wet. Thankfully, a bedside lamp allowed me to see every line in his stomach, every flexed muscle as his hands worked their magic all over my body until he tossed the towel to the side.

Tearing my bikini bottoms off, Parker groaned as he looked at me.

"You are goddamn perfect, Delaney."

With the same speed and efficiency as he'd dried me, Parker did the same to himself, taking off his wet bathing suit and tossing it onto the towel.

I looked down.

Very erect. "You are kinda perfect yourself," I murmured a second before finding myself carried once again, this time to the bed.

Putting me down, Parker climbed in next to me. As he pulled me toward him for a hard, demanding kiss, I wasn't surprised when his hand began at my shoulder and moved down, cupping one breast before going lower, and lower.

Slipping one finger inside, he began to move it to the same rhythm as his tongue. Soon, a second finger joined in the fun and Parker had me writhing beneath his movements. I didn't want to know how he was so skilled at this.

"Mmmm." I couldn't get enough of him, pushing my hips against his fingers.

"Do you remember," he said, breaking the kiss and whispering into my ear, "what I told you in the hot tub?"

Swallowing, I made a sound that was maybe sort of a "uh huh" but more just a moan.

"Good, because you are so fucking wet for me, Delaney, that I'm pretty sure three times is just going to be a start. I'm going to make you come so many times tonight that you'll wonder how such a thing was even possible."

I was so close to number one already.

"Parker," I said softly.

"Louder," he said, his thumb circling as his fingers worked me.

"Parker, please." My hips thrusted up toward him.

So close.

"Louder, cupcake," he whispered.

That did it. Exploding into his hand, I let go so completely that, if we did have neighbors, they'd have heard me call his name. That he did that with his fingers wasn't something I could comprehend at the moment. Kissing me as he pulled out, Parker's lips soft and soothing now to match the ebbing throbs that were fading quickly, he suddenly broke away again.

"I'm glad you remember," he said, sliding down in between my legs. "Look at you. Dear God, those breasts. And hips." His hands moved to each body part he talked about. "Your legs are so smooth, just like this," he said, leaning down and kissing me at the top of my bikini line.

"Where did you come from?" I asked as his kisses moved lower, and lower.

"Hamlin. New York." Another kiss. "Pretty sure I told you that," he teased, his hands moving to the inside of my thighs.

They paused. "If I remember correctly, I promised to make you come this way only after you begged me for it."

Remembering his exact words on the ski lift, I asked anyway. "Really? I don't recall."

"I do," he said, Parker's voice low and husky. "Say please, Delaney."

His mouth was no more than an inch or two from me. Seeing him between my legs this way, the aftereffects of an orgasm that he'd brought on with his damn fingers... I almost said the word. But didn't, just to torment him back.

Smiling, I lifted my chin in the air and braced myself for his reaction.

"If you want me to bury my face in this sweet pussy of yours and only come out until the last time you called my name sounds like a whisper... say please."

Man, he was so dirty.

I loved it. Absolutely, unequivocally loved it.

Rather than waiting for Parker to pull my legs wide, like he'd promised, I did it for him. Looking down, he groaned. Closed his eyes. And then played dirty.

Parker's tongue started in the corner of his mouth and, as he opened his eyes and stared directly at me, it glided across his lower lip.

Enough was enough. The sight of him between me, licking his damn lips...

"Please."

Making good on his promise, Parker pushed my legs so they bent at the knees and opened me even wider. And then absolutely plunged his tongue inside me without warning. It was only a second later that he withdrew and began to use his tongue to play me like a fiddle. Gripping the sheets, I tossed my head back, unable to watch him anymore. I couldn't possibly be ready to come so quickly already.

But I was.

His tongue pressed, circled and licked in ways I never even thought possible. "Parker, please," I said, not caring if I begged. Wanting to. Wanting him to make me come again. "Holy shit, are you serious right now?" I managed.

In response, he increased the pressure, his thumbs rubbing circles on my thighs as his tongue absolutely ravished me. Lifting my hips, I asked for more without words.

I couldn't talk anymore.

My legs began to shake. The tension built and built, and the only thing I could hear was the pounding of my own heart. And maybe the moans of pleasure that may have included a few more cries of Parker's name.

And then everything came apart. I squeezed my eyes shut, waiting for the comedown that took longer than usual. I had never, ever, ever come that hard in my life.

When I finally did open my eyes, Parker was gone. It only took a second for me to realize he was reaching for a condom on the nightstand. I watched as he unwrapped it and slowly covered himself, not something that I'd usually associate with being erotic, but this time?

It was the way he looked at me.

"Now that," he said, climbing back into the bed, "was hot."

Words escaped me.

"Let me try to remember what I promised you. Oh, yeah, I never did get to finish, did I?"

I shook my head. "No. You didn't."

"What I meant to say was that the third time will put the first two to shame. That I would fuck you like you've never been fucked in your life."

I couldn't breathe.

"Delaney?"

"Uh huh?"

"I'm waiting."

He was waiting for me?

"For?"

"For you to give me permission."

"To fuck me?" I managed, not usually one to use that particular term. Parker apparently brought out my dirty-talking side too. Kind of.

"Yes, cupcake. To fuck you. And then later, to make love to you."

As if I could speak. I nodded my head, and Parker came down toward me.

22

PARKER

This was dangerous.

My desire to have Delaney think of tonight during her every waking moment, and sleeping ones too, was trouble. Even recognizing it, I couldn't stop. I wanted her to crave me the same way as I craved her. Every second we were together, I wanted more.

More time to talk.

More time to get to know her.

More kisses.

More of this.

The second she nodded, I moved between her, guiding myself into her. All day I imagined this, being inside of her. Pleasing her.

"Fuck." I couldn't help it. We just fit together so damn perfectly.

Delaney grabbed my shoulders as I eased all the way into her. Kissing her, I stayed that way until I was sure she'd adjusted to me. And then I began to move. Slowly at first, picking up the pace as she met each and every thrust.

Slipping my hand between us, I did the one thing that would ensure she didn't forget this anytime soon. Lifting myself up, I moved in and out, rubbing her with my thumb and staring directly into those beautiful eyes of hers.

"This is only the beginning," I said, changing up the pace. "I really hope you didn't plan on getting any sleep tonight."

Her mouth opened, but Delaney didn't say anything. Instead she watched me, meeting every thrust.

"I want you to try to get out of this bed in the morning," I said, moving faster and faster. "But your legs will barely support you. I'm going to fuck you in every position, and just when you think we're done, I'm going to fuck you some more."

"Oh my God. Parker. When you say things like that..."

Our pace was indescribable. Two people had never moved in such perfect rhythm before. Remembering she was unlikely to come that way alone, I made sure not to forget to use my fingers to bring Delaney to climax.

"This time, though, I plan to come with you. The very second you feel it." We moved faster and faster. "I want you to tell me. Say it, cupcake. Tell me when you come."

"I..."

"How does that feel? Do you like it like this?" I slowed down. "Or like this?"

"Both. Both. Parker, I can't."

"What can't you do? Come for me? Sure you can. Do it. Come with me, Delaney."

It was as if something had held her back until that second, but Delaney suddenly decided to let it all go. We moved together almost wildly until she called my name. Encouraging her, telling Delaney she could say anything, scream as loud as she wanted, she began to tense.

I removed my hand, pushed deep inside her, and together

we both let go. Every muscle in my body tensed as I held myself over her. Our mouths found each other's as waves of pleasure came crashing down.

I'd wanted to give her a night to remember, but ended up doing the same for myself. It was as if we had been intimate many times before. There was no awkwardness. No apologies. Just the two of us letting our instincts take over.

Rolling to my back, as spent as I'd promised Delaney she would be, I tried to catch my breath, finally looking over at her.

"I feel like I need a cigarette."

"Do you smoke?" I asked.

"No. Do you?"

"No, but I will partake in the occasional cigar under the right circumstances."

Not wanting to move but knowing I had to clean up, I managed to slide off the bed and do just that, coming back into the bedroom to see Delaney propped on one elbow. Gloriously naked. An absolute masterpiece.

"I wish you could see yourself right now," I said, joining her in the bed. Together we managed to get under the comforter and sheets. Pulling her into my side, I took a deep breath, content.

"Three times. Right in a row. I think that's a record for me."

I smiled into the darkness. "We're just getting started. I hope you realize that."

"Tonight, you mean?"

I shifted to the side to see her face, unable to read her expression.

"Tonight, yes. But maybe after tonight, too?"

Whether or not it was the right answer, I wasn't certain. All I could do was give her honesty. And the honest to God's truth was, I had no idea what was going to happen next.

"We've already established," I continued, "that we're two people who are broken. Relationship wise. So maybe we can be broken together?"

"What does that mean, exactly?"

Laughing, I admitted, "I have no idea."

Delaney smiled. "I'll tell you one thing, you certainly have my number, that's for sure."

"Oh, yeah? Glad to hear it."

Leaning my head down, since Delaney seemed to like when I whispered into her ear, I said, "How about you tell me what you like the most, and I will do it again. And again. And again. And again."

"Seriously?" She laughed. "How many times do you think you can actually get me to come in one night?"

"I'm not sure," I said, spinning us around so Delaney was on top of me. "But I'm thinking it might be fun to find out."

* * *

Seven times.

Delaney claimed it was a record for her, and I believed her. When I woke up, I hadn't wanted to leave the bed. Knowing she wasn't an early riser, after watching her sleep in my arms for a while, I eventually got up, thinking to start cleaning out the house.

After making coffee, I tossed food we hadn't used and packed the rest in the car. After I loaded and started the dishwasher, the only thing left to do was put those away when they were finished and strip our bed.

"Look at you, Mr. Morning Guy. Penny for your thoughts?"

I'd been staring out at the mountain, clear skies leaving

more than five or six inches of snow by the looks of it. Turning, I watched as Delaney poured herself a cup of coffee.

"I was thinking we'd have to strip the bed. But now I'm thinking of stripping you instead."

She laughed. "There is absolutely no chance my body could handle what might happen if you did."

Smiling, I asked if she was sore.

"Yes. And you don't look very remorseful about that either."

"I'm not," I admitted.

Delaney joined me.

"That was, without a doubt, the greatest night of sex I've ever had in my life."

I just couldn't quit smiling. "Glad to hear it." I leaned over to kiss her. It was meant to be a quick kiss, but her lips were too damn soft and inviting. A few minutes later, pulling away, I took a sip of coffee.

She cleared her throat.

I nearly spit out the coffee laughing. She was very predictable, my redheaded bedmate.

"I knew not answering would get a rise out of you."

"Did you now?"

"I did. And it was unequivocally the greatest night of sex I've ever had too," I added finally. Then, to be certain she knew it was true, "Delaney. I'm serious. We really are incredible together."

"In bed," she clarified.

That's not what I meant, but I didn't want to scare her. Despite last night, she was still very much scarred from her last relationship.

"Sure," I agreed without much conviction. "Honestly, I had a great time yesterday. And last night."

"Me too."

We stood beside each other for a few minutes, no words needed. I assumed Delaney was thinking about some of the same things I was. No matter how things went between us, I had a feeling I'd be thinking about our night together for a very, very long time.

"I don't want to leave," she said finally, echoing my thoughts.

"It is an incredible house," I said, looking around and finally landing my gaze on a not-so-pleased Delaney. At least, she was pretending to be displeased. I was pretty sure she could tell I was teasing.

"Exactly," she said, her tone dry. "The house is just *too amazing*. My thoughts exactly."

Laughing, I winked. "Seriously though, it's a great house."

"Speaking of the house... when is that workshop in Rochester you mentioned?"

"I think it's next weekend. It could be filled already. Why?"

"You should check it out."

"Maybe I will." I took a step toward the closest wall, running a hand over the wood. "There are a lot of benefits to being in log cabin construction."

"Such as?"

"It's a niche market which means I wouldn't be taking business away from my boss."

"The one you don't like?"

I peeked over at Delaney, who took a sip of coffee, looking as innocent as can be.

"Yeah," I admitted. "That one. He's a better guy than he is a boss, if you know what I mean."

"I totally do. Some people are great to hang out with, not so great to work for."

"Exactly."

"What are the other benefits?"

"It's a specialized expertise with higher margins since log cabins are considered premium properties. They're also usually built using sustainable materials, which is good for the environment."

"Sounds to me like you should go to that workshop."

I took my hand off the wall and closed the distance between us. Without a word, I took her coffee cup and put both hers and my own on the closest table. Making my way back to her, I wrapped my hands around the back of her neck, pulling Delaney close.

The kiss was slow. Deliberate.

It told Delaney how glad I was to be here with her. How much I didn't want to leave. How much I'd enjoyed our night together. With her arms around my waist, like before, we fit together as if Delaney and I were made for each other.

Never stay the night.

We made it a rule with good reason. If the goal was not to fall for a woman, not to fall in love, not to get married, spending an entire night pleasing and holding each other like we had was, without a doubt, counterproductive. At the time, I hadn't hesitated. Seeing the dark hole my mother had fallen down after my father's betrayal, pretending to be fine when we knew she wasn't, had affected me deeply.

I shook off the memory.

"It's hard to believe," Delaney said when we stopped, "that I'm kissing you, with that view, but soon I'll be standing behind a counter for eight hours with probably very few customers, bored to tears."

"Snow?" I asked.

"Yeah. You'd think living in upstate New York people would be a bit hardier. More than an inch or two, the place is dead."

"They've gotten spoiled around the lake. Back home, no one would blink at three inches."

"Why does it snow less on the lake anyway?"

"It has to do with the lake temperature and moisture absorption. And wind patterns too."

"Interesting."

"You know what's even more interesting?"

"No," she said, her arms tightening around me, as if I'd planned on going anywhere. "What?"

"You. Everything about you interests me, Delaney. Let me bring you dinner tonight. Keep you company."

She made a face. "You really want to spend your night in an empty pharmacy?"

"It won't be empty. You'll be there. So yes. I do. Very much."

23

DELANEY

Done.

I put the bracelet on myself. It was easy enough to make, just some leather strips, stainless steel clips and beads. With my signature boho vibes and adjustable closure, it was almost an identical one to Pia's and ready to be shipped to her former guest.

Taking it off, I stood up and stretched, heading from my second-floor studio to the kitchen for a water refill. As I suspected, it had only taken about an hour to make, so there was plenty of time before I headed down to Heritage Hill.

For Taco Tuesday.

With Parker.

It wasn't lost on either of us that this would be the fourth day in a row we were together. Bringing dinner last night, as promised, he sat with me until closing. Just as I'd suspected, there were few orders and even fewer customers.

Did I really want to do that job for the rest of my life?

The answer was almost as scary as what was happening with me and Parker. I went from a red light immediately to green, skipping yellow altogether. That night at Crystal Peak was like a switch being turned on inside of me after months of hurt and healing.

Of course my friends wanted to know everything, and while I didn't tell Pia or Jules about Parker's penchant for dirty talk, I may have said something about that night being the best sex of my life. Only because it was totally true.

Heading back upstairs, I stared at my supplies for a few minutes before cleaning. Parker had signed up for his workshop and was heading to Rochester next weekend. I could tell he was really excited about it with good reason. Although he'd always planned to start his own construction company in Cedar Falls, Parker admitted last night he had felt stuck, unsure where to start. He volunteered to help Mason renovate Heritage Hill partly to get a big job under his belt that wasn't associated with the company he worked for. And even though he was moving in the right direction, he never really saw a clear path forward.

Until now.

Niching into log cabin home construction might be, as Parker had put it, "his ticket out."

What was my ticket out? Could I follow in his footsteps and take such a risk? Probably not. Home building was a viable career. Art, as my parents often reminded me, was not. Plus, I had so many years of schooling, and money invested, in my pharmacy degree. And a job that Mom said was a "once-in-a-lifetime opportunity," since the turnover rate of pharmacists in Cedar Falls was next to nil.

Shaking my head, I cleaned up and headed into the bathroom to shower. It was only a few blocks' walk through the town square and down the hill to the lake, to Heritage Hill, but I needed to leave early to stop at Casa Di Vino. Walking into the empty wine store, I empathized with poor Emilio, the owner. He looked positively bored, staring at a magazine of some sort, though he didn't seem to actually be reading it.

"Slow day, huh?"

"Days," he clarified. "Not even foot traffic. You'd think we had two feet out there."

"Busy on the weekend?"

"I was," he said. "No one wanted to get stuck in a storm without their favorite vino."

"A fate worse than death," I agreed. Heading to the back to grab a bottle of Pia's favorite, Pinot Noir, I prepared to be chastised by the Italian immigrant who had owned this shop for as long as I could remember.

"Willamette Valley Pinot is good, *mia cara*, but I have something better."

His family still owned a vineyard in "the old country" as Emilio said, and it was excellent, but this wasn't for me. "I'm heading down the hill," I said. "This is for Pia."

"Ahh, she's a stubborn one too. Perfect for the Bennett boy," he said, ringing me out.

I loved the fact that he called Mason, a thirty-two-year-old former Army Ranger, "the Bennett boy." "They really are perfect for each other," I agreed.

"What about you, Miss Thorton? Do you have a perfect man, or woman?" he quickly added. "Don't mean to discriminate. I try to keep up with the times."

"You're doing great," I assured him. "But no, I don't have a perfect man. I mean"—I thought about that for a second—"I'm not sure if I do or not."

Emilio's brows raised. "We aren't talking about Makis?"

"No, we're not. But the fact that you know that tells me how horrible he really was for me."

"Signoria Delaney, any man who makes you question your-self is not the one for you."

"You could have told me much sooner," I teased.

"Would you have listened?"

"No," I said. "I wouldn't."

"So who's the new guy?"

I didn't want to define us yet. Not after less than a week. "He's so new I don't want to jinx it."

Emilio's eyes narrowed. "I know him."

"It's Cedar Falls. Of course you know him," I teased.

He sat back down on his stool, crossed his arms, and looked at me as if he knew something I didn't.

"Emilio Russo?" I tried, knowing I wouldn't get anywhere. He called Pia and Mason stubborn, but it was a fact that, of all the store owners in town, no one dug in his heels more than this guy. He was easy-going in a lot of ways, but his ideas were his own and no one would tell him otherwise.

"Fine," I said. "Be mysterious."

"Tell Pia and Mason I said *buongiorno*."

"Will do." With narrowed eyes and a look that apparently did not move Emilio to confess what he'd written on that scrap of paper, I made my way from the door.

"*Ciao*," I said, used to his standard greeting, and parting.

"*Ciao, ciao*," he replied as I opened the door and left, heading down the hill.

Do you have a perfect man?

There really was no such thing, but as far as Parker went, he was pretty damn close. Sure, he had hangups because of his father. And if I'd given a list of qualities in a boyfriend, "extreme outdoorsman" would not have been one of them. My idea of camping started and stopped at making s'mores by the fire, followed by running water to take a shower and a bed with a big fluffy pillow. But he was also kind, thoughtful, beyond good-looking... and then there was the whole bedroom skill-set thing. I literally could not get Sunday night out of my head, and probably never would for the rest of my life.

And yet I'd thought Makis was pretty darn awesome until he'd torn my heart into a million pieces. But I wouldn't dwell on that. I resolved to put him firmly in the past, and that was what I would do.

I knocked at the door of the "house" side of Heritage Hill, the inn and original structure attached but completely separate from the addition where the boys, and Pia, lived, and it was less than thirty seconds when the door opened.

"Hey, Delaney. For not seeing you," Beck said, opening the door wide, "almost ever, this is like the third time in a week. Come on in."

"I hope you're not complaining," I said, heading inside. The smell of tacos made my mouth water. "No work tonight?"

"Not at all. Off," he said. "Working two doubles in the next three days."

"Ouch. I know how that feels."

We walked toward the kitchen. Even though this part of the inn was an add-on, it had the same feel as the original. Heritage Hill was more like a mini castle than it was a house, and since Mason's dad passed and he and the guys had been renovating it, the place looked amazing, a combination of grandiosity that was the manor house but with modern B&B vibes.

"There's my girl," Pia said when we walked in.

Unfortunately, Parker was nowhere to be found.

He'd first mentioned Taco Tuesday last night, and when I texted Pia to tell her, she had been thrilled that I would be coming.

"This is for you," I said, handing her the wine.

"Delaney Montana Thorton. You did not have to bring this. You're family here."

"Montana?"

The voice went right through me, giving me a tingling sensation from my shoulders down to my toes. If I closed my eyes, I could see him positioned above me, Parker's tone low and intimate. Just like that.

Turning, I wondered what I'd been thinking when we'd had lunch together. Did I really believe it was possible to resist him?

A moss-green long-sleeve shirt, cuffs rolled to his elbows, made his eyes look more green than hazel. His hair still damp, Parker was... perfect.

There is no such thing as a perfect man.

Except the evidence standing in front of me suggested otherwise.

"My parents conceived me on a hunting trip to Montana. Mom wasn't supposed to go but Dad's friend canceled last minute."

He walked toward me. "I didn't know your dad was a hunter?"

"I didn't mention it?"

"No," he said, stopping short of me. Apparently we weren't at the "greet with a kiss" stage yet. Which should not have disappointed me since the last thing I wanted was a full-blown relationship.

"I imagine you are?" I asked him.

Mason snorted. "Deer. Turkey. Bear. Archery. Rifle. You name a hunting season and Parker's into it."

"You'd get along great with my dad."

"Would like to meet him sometime."

Our eyes met, and held. He fired the first shot, so I'd just match his energy.

"That could be arranged."

Beck cleared his throat. "If you two lovebirds could step aside," he said, trying to reach the island, "I was just making a taco station."

"Margarita?" Pia asked, as she was clearly in charge of drinks.

"Duh," I said, standing off to the side. Didn't want to get between Beck and his tacos.

Parker leaned down toward my ear, which was when I knew I was in for it.

"I didn't ask to come home with you last night, cupcake. Thought you could use a break. But I'm asking now if you'll let me take you home later?"

As Parker went, his words were much milder than expected.

"Sure," I said quietly, unsure why he'd whispered it.

"Good," he said, still in my ear. "Because I do enjoy tacos but am more looking forward to dessert."

Hello, Parker.

"What are you two whispering about over there?" Pia teased, coming toward me with a margarita.

Parker stood up straight as I took the drink. "Trade secrets, my child."

"Well, Mr. Mysterious, the more important question is, do you want a margarita?"

"Why not? I like to live on the edge."

"Look at that," Beck said, apparently finished with his taco station just as Mason poured a pan of beef into a bowl on the counter. "Mr. Miller Light, expanding his horizons."

"I drink other stuff too."

"Sure, like Coors Light. Sometimes Ultra when you really want your beer to taste like water."

"He had wine at Crystal Peak," I said, trying to defend

Parker. Apparently, it backfired. Both Mason and Beck froze and stared at Parker, who shrugged.

"What? I've been known to drink wine on occasion."

"Oh, yeah, what occasion is that?"

"To answer your question," Parker said to Pia, ignoring his friends, "yes, please. With salt."

"Coming right up."

We drank margaritas. Ate tacos. Laughed. The guys taunted and teased each other mercilessly as if they were brothers.

When Parker and I reached for a tortilla chip at the same time and our fingers touched, I had visions of last weekend. When he looked at me from across the room where he and Pia made a second round of margaritas, I had visions of last weekend.

Pretty much all night, anytime we got close, I had... you guessed it... visions of last weekend. Our chemistry was undeniable.

Pia asked if I needed to hit the ladies' room.

"There's one toilet," Mason said.

"Right. We're close," she responded, grabbing my hand.

The second we were alone, Pia gushed, "Delaney, holy crap. It is ten times more intense than you described. He cannot stop looking at you."

"The feeling is mutual," I said.

We stood outside the bathroom, speaking in hushed voices like two teenage girls. I couldn't help feeling giddy, though, at the thought of Parker coming home with me tonight.

"He's taking me home," I added.

"Taking you home? Or staying over?"

"Good question. Hopefully, the latter," I admitted.

Pia's smile could not have been any bigger. "Makis who?"

24

PARKER

"What's this for?" Beck asked as I handed him a hundred bucks.

"Sunday. Tonight. Whatever. Add it to the kitty."

"Tonight?" Mason leaned against the kitchen counter. "You staying at her place?"

"Hopefully," I said. "I can argue Sunday didn't count, but tonight will. And I honestly don't give a shit what you two assholes have to say about it."

Mason threw up his hands. "Not casting stones here."

"I am." Beck pocketed the cash. "You stay the night, things happen."

"Maybe I don't care." As soon as the words came out of my mouth, I realized how true they were. I didn't care. Not with Delaney. If my choices were keeping her at arm's length or risk getting close, I'd be picking door number two.

"Maybe you should."

It was Beck's tone that got me. He was rarely serious. About anything.

He shrugged. "Just sayin'... you remember the reason we took it? New relationships cloud the true story. Not one of us with parents who weren't devastated in some way because of their significant other. And they all started out"—he waved his arm to Mason—"like him. Or you, from the looks of it."

Mason opened his mouth to argue with him, but I stopped him. Arguing with Beck was useless. Forget about the fact that, before meeting Delaney, I'd have agreed with him. Wholeheartedly. "In other news, I signed up for a log cabin building workshop in Rochester next weekend."

"Oh, yeah?" Mason took a swig of beer, side-eyeing Beck but playing along with me. "What are you thinking?"

"That it could be a good niche. I wouldn't be directly competing with Rich, and the margins are high on log cabin homes. The big question is the market in our area."

"Who gives a shit about Rich?" Beck asked. "He's a dickhead anyway."

"Maybe," I agreed. "But he's still the biggest construction game in town."

Mason pulled out his phone, looking at it. Putting his beer down, he pushed himself away from the counter. "Guest is locked out." He rolled his eyes. "Be right back."

There were spare keys to all the rooms hidden in various places, but that was exactly why changing the doors to keypads was Parker's next job. The fact that Mason's dad had never had a problem with getting broken into, despite the fact that the hidden keys weren't a huge secret around town, was shocking.

"Log cabin construction." Beck put the last of the taco dinner leftovers in the fridge. "Interesting. Do you need a special permit for that?"

"No," I said. "But a portfolio wouldn't hurt. That'll probably be the biggest issue. I may have an idea on how to tackle that too."

"Do tell."

"Yes, do tell," Pia said as she and Delaney came back into the kitchen. Hopefully that would ensure no more talk about the pact. Remembering the exact discussion that had led to it gave me a queasy feeling in my stomach. "What are we telling?"

"Boring stuff," I said.

"Parker's finally thinking to pull the trigger on his own business, niching down into log cabin home construction," Beck said.

Pia smiled. "I may have heard something about that already."

As usual, Delaney was smiling. The term "sunny disposition" was invented for her.

"Oh, yeah?" I asked, looking at Delaney. "Are you the culprit here?"

"Maybe," she said cheekily.

"What else do you ladies talk about, I wonder?"

"I can guarantee it's not the same thing as you boys." Pia turned to Delaney. "I've overheard more of their discussions living here than I care to admit."

"First of all"—Beck closed the dishwasher—"men, not boys. Second of all"—he appeared genuinely confused—"you all don't talk about sex?"

Delaney pressed her lips tight together, trying not to laugh.

"Of course we do. I was talking about the other 80 percent of your conversations." Pia looked at me. "Aka, sports."

"But you do talk about sex? Among your own kind?" Beck asked.

The brother/sister rapport between Pia and Beck was unique.

"Our own kind? We are women, Beck. Not an entirely different species."

He snorted. "I'm not sure about that one."

"What has you so confused?" I asked. Beck's face scrunched up in mock concentration. He really was one of a kind. I could somewhat see why every female in Cedar Falls lost their mind over him. Besides being good-looking, he was endearing, in an airheaded, surfer dude kind of way. At least, that was how he presented. Very few people knew that he was anything but. If I had to put money on it, I'd put his IQ above even Cole's, although no one who had met both of them would ever believe it. Beck was mostly show. The guy masked a lot of shit he never wanted to talk about.

Since I hadn't stared at her in all of about the last two minutes, I peeked over at Delaney. Sitting at the kitchen island sipping her margarita, she was listening to Beck and Pia. What would she do if I walked up to her, pushed her hair to the side and kissed her neck? All night I wanted to touch her so badly, but I didn't know if she was ready for public displays of affection in front of friends. Despite Crystal Peak, there was a hesitancy about her still that most likely related back to the ex. I got it, not wanting to jump in with both feet. On the other hand, staying away from her wasn't an option for me.

She looked over.

I lifted the margarita glass to my lips, made sure neither Pia nor Beck were looking, and stuck my tongue out, just slightly. Twisting the glass to where salt still remained, I licked it off and then took a sip.

Delaney swallowed. Shifted on her stool.

Smiling, liking this game, I put my drink on the counter and pulled out my phone.

Hi there, cupcake.

I watched as she pulled her phone out of the back pocket of her jeans.

Hi there, yourself.

Having a good time?

I am. Are you?

Yes.

I looked up. She did the same. The others didn't seem to notice us thanks to their ongoing conversation.

Although, I can think of something better than tacos and margaritas.

While she read my text and typed a response, I picked up my drink, took a sip, and pretended to care about what the others were saying. In truth, I wasn't hearing any of their conversation. The prospect of leaving here, imminently, with Delaney, over-rode all other thoughts.

I put the drink back down and glanced at her response.

What could possibly be better than tacos and margaritas?

I wasn't certain if Delaney liked her texts dirty too, but I was about to find out.

You. Specifically you pinned beneath me as I lick your nipples the way I just did that salt.

Thankfully, I didn't need to wait long for her reaction. The second she finished reading my text, her head snapped up.

"Are you two seriously texting each other?"

Leave it to Beck to be discreet.

"Don't know what gave you that idea," I said, taking a sip of my drink.

"Leave them alone." Pia swatted Beck's shoulder.

Mason grinned. "I think you two make a cute couple," he said.

Sometimes, I like the "old" Mason. The grumpier one that didn't talk as much, pre-Pia. The one that didn't use the word "cute." This one was foreign to me.

"Oh, so now that you're out of the pact, you're trying to recruit members of the 'anti-bachelor pact'?" Beck frowned.

"There's no such thing," I said dryly.

"Whatever. Traitors," he mumbled under his breath.

"Now Beck," Pia said, as if speaking to a child. "You can't possibly wish for Mason and me not to have met."

"Obviously not. You're the best thing that ever happened to him," he said, in a moment of rare Beck sincerity. "There's always an exception to the rule."

"Awww." Pia pretended to sooth the shoulder she'd swatted as Mason rolled his eyes.

With the others distracted, I finished my drink and picked my phone back up.

> Speaking of me ravishing that incredible body of yours...

Delaney looked down at her phone, then back up at me. I nodded toward the door. In response, she downed the rest of her drink.

I laughed loud enough for the others to stop talking and look my way. Coughing, in a poor attempt at recovery, I managed, "Thirsty?"

"Extremely." Delaney was about to crack up but somehow held it together. "And a little tired, to be honest."

"Must be something in the air. I'm feeling a little..." I hesi-tated. Summoned a straight face and finished. "Sleepy, too."

"Sure. Something is in the air, alright," Pia teased.

"It's been real," I said, heading toward Delaney. "But I'm walking her home."

"Thank you so much," she said. "I'm so glad to have finally made a Taco Tuesday."

"Anytime." Pia gave her a kiss on the cheek. "Thanks for the wine."

"My pleasure. See you, Mason. Beck."

After goodbyes, I grabbed our coats by the door, more than ready to finally get a chance to touch Delaney, when she stopped me.

"Before we go..."

I waited, staring at her lips, not able to stand it any longer. Reaching for her, I closed the distance between us, pulling her toward me. Our mouths met as if we'd been kissing each other forever. Fitting perfectly together, only the thought of getting her home made me stop. Catch a breath.

"Yes, cupcake?"

She smiled. "I was thinking, since you have to work early tomorrow, that maybe... maybe you'd want to grab... I don't know. A toothbrush. Work clothes. Maybe leave from my place?"

Hell, yeah. "Are you asking me to stay the night?"

"I guess I am."

Without answering, I bolted from the foyer toward the stairs. "Be right back," I said, heading toward my bedroom and putting together an overnight bag in record time.

Did I care if Delaney saw how glad I was she asked?

No.

Was I going to play bullshit cat and mouse games with her?

Also no.

Was it a good idea to spend the night with her after we just did so two days ago?

Another no.

But sometimes, you just had to say "fuck it" and follow your gut... for better or worse.

25

DELANEY

It was a five-minute drive to my house from the inn. I had on a bulky winter coat. Jeans. There were so many reasons that Parker's hand should not be down my pants at the moment, except... that was where we were.

And honestly, it was one of the hottest things ever. The fact that he didn't want to wait to please me, which was exactly what he'd said the second his truck began to warm up and we drove away. One second, he was pulling out of the inn's driveway, the next he'd reached across my lap and said, "Help me please you," as he pushed aside my coat and began to unbutton my jeans.

While driving.

"Um, maybe you should concentrate on the road?"

"And the two other people driving around Cedar Falls at the moment? No, thanks. I'd rather concentrate on you."

Thankfully, he'd done both.

And now we were just a few blocks away as my left hand gripped his jacket sleeve and the other tried to clasp onto the door but couldn't find any leverage.

"Parker." I glanced over at him. Though he was actually

watching the road, he also must have been acutely aware that he was about to make me come. The smile on this face was 100 percent "cat that ate the canary."

"Parker," I said again. "How?" I stopped. Not wanting the answer. His fingers were absolutely magical. "Jesus." I pressed my hips into him, Parker's two fingers alternatively rubbing and circling my clit before plunging into me and somehow, even at this angle, finding my g-spot. His arm was stretched clear across the center console, but he looked as comfortable as a light breeze on a summer's day.

"There is no one," he said. "Just you. Your pleasure. The way you call my name. Can you do that for me, Delaney? Call my name as you let go of all your inhibitions? For me?"

He pulled into an empty spot on my street, put the truck into park and then leaned over toward me, watching me.

It was too much.

His words.

His expression.

His fingers.

"Parker…"

"That's it. Louder."

I was going to come. And did. Pulsing around his fingers, I called his name again, watching him watching me. Squeezing my eyes shut for just a second, I let the aftereffects caress my body as Parker removed his hand.

"Can we maybe stay here," I said, beyond content in his warm truck. "Maybe take a little nap?"

"Not a chance," he said, turning off the engine.

"Mmmm," I groaned, not moving, even when Parker got out of the truck and came around to my side. A blast of cold hit me as he opened the door. And as quickly as he'd brought me from Heritage Hill to climax, I was scooped out of the truck into his arms. Squealing, I reached behind his neck, holding on. "What are you..."

Kicking the door shut, Parker proceeded to carry me up the stairs of my house, only letting me down at the door. Laughing so hard I couldn't find my keys, I thought for a second we might freeze to death.

"Got 'em."

Once inside, I turned on a lamp and knelt down to light the fire, wishing for the millionth time it was electric.

"I got it," Parker said, taking over.

Glad to let him, I scurried around, lighting candles and tidying up a bit. "Make yourself at home."

"Nice place," he said, finishing the fire and looking around casually as if he'd not just gotten me off on the five-minute ride here. Trying not to dwell on that, or this extreme need I had to be close to him again, to touch him like I'd wanted to do all night, I hung up my coat and asked if he wanted a drink.

"I'm good," he said, picking up a picture from the fireplace mantel. "So this is the family?"

I headed back into my small but comfortable living room. "Yep. Mom, Dad, brother."

"I know your mom is a dentist and father is an engineer, but what does your brother do? Is he married?"

"Nope. My mother worries it might never happen... Just turned thirty-five. He moved to Rochester for work, also an engineer like Dad, but mechanical. He's currently living the work hard, play hard lifestyle."

"I know a few guys like that."

"Beck?"

"And Cole. Mason too until last year." He put down the picture.

"I don't think he's as opposed to it as you guys are, bachelor pact and all. Just hasn't found the right woman."

"That pact," he said as I walked toward him, "was just a silly college game." Reaching for me, Parker pulled me into his arms.

"Seems like Beck still takes it seriously."

He smoothed back my hair so it was completely off my face. Cupping my cheeks in his hands, Parker stared into my eyes.

"He's not in any rush to settle down. Cole either."

I almost said, "And you?" but thought better of it. I knew the answer and didn't need to press. We weren't even officially dating, and the last thing I wanted was another broken heart. And yet...

"Which of them do you think we crack first?" I asked, hoping Parker hadn't noticed my hesitation.

"Whew, that's a tough one. Is neither an option?"

I would have answered, but Parker had leaned down to kiss me, and I was ready. I wasn't sure if his need to touch me was because of having been denied it all night, like mine. We'd really have to discuss that.

Later.

At the moment we were too busy tearing our clothes off. That wasn't just an expression either. I'd never gotten undressed more quickly than when Parker began to unbutton his shirt.

"For the record, if wearing your shirt sleeves rolled up like that is a habit of yours, I'm here for it."

"Oh, yeah?" he asked, tossing boots, socks and jeans to the side.

"Yeah." I was down to bra and underwear, the nicest ones I owned. And it seemed Parker appreciated the fact that this black lace set was particularly sexy.

"Dear lord," he said, pausing for the first time since he'd removed his shirt. "Would you look at that? Perfection."

It was just a compliment. Easily enough given. I'd learned actions were more important than words when it came to men. But somehow, none of that mattered. Parker's sincerity had to be real.

"Thank you," I said, having worked on my ability to accept a compliment without qualifying it. "You're not so bad yourself."

He pulled me to him. "Let me finish this for you."

Unlike the frantic pace we'd set removing our clothes, Parker reached behind my back, unclasped my bra, and pulled the straps off slowly with his thumbs. Making a sound that confirmed he very much liked what he saw, Parker tossed the bra aside, cupping both breasts in his hands.

We stood like that in front of the fire, kissing... touching... exploring, for longer than I would have expected when we'd so hastily removed our clothing. Almost as if he revered me, Parker knelt down and looked up, pausing.

It was the single sexiest thing he'd done yet, Parker's hands running up my calves as he remained on his knees, watching me. I wanted to say something, but had no words. Maybe it was better this way, without them.

Reaching up, he pulled down the black lace underwear bit by bit, only standing when they were completely off me. I did the same to him, springing Parker free, verifying that he was very much ready for me.

"I can't decide," he said, guiding me to the couch, "if I want to spend the next hour kissing every inch of your body before making love to you on that fur rug of yours beside the fire..."

He spun us around so that Parker's back was to the couch. "Or if I should sit on the couch and have you straddle me, in complete control, and let you have your way with me."

As always, his words got to me, making me forget everything

but the visions he painted in my mind. Feeling saucy, I pushed on his chest. "I choose number two."

"I need to—"

Knowing what he was going to say, I stopped him.

"I'm on the pill."

Our eyes met and locked.

Parker sat. I straddled him. And just like that, we were back to not being able to get enough of each other. Not wanting to wait any longer, I guided him into me, already wet and ready to take his full length, and just as he'd said, I had my way with him.

Parker's hands rested on my hips, his fingers digging into the flesh there with the sweetest sort of pressure as I moved up and down. Using his shoulders for leverage, I moved alternatively fast and slow. Circled and paused. Every move was mine to choose, a heady sort of pleasure so different than any of the other times we'd been together.

With the fire at my back, Parker's expression one of awe and emotion, I was a goddess in that moment. Or at least I felt like one as I tossed my head back and let myself go.

"You are spectacular."

His voice, his words... I kissed him. Ravaged him. Before long, our bodies moved in perfect rhythm at a pace that would be impossible to keep. Parker seemed to sense I was close.

"Come on, cupcake. Together."

Knowing what he meant, I moved my hips just the right way and cried out, Parker thrusting his hips up to me harder than he had all night.

Maybe it was the control. Maybe knowing we had no barrier between us. The whole night, wanting to touch him. The fire. The look in his eyes. I wasn't sure. But something had shifted between us, and in the aftermath, before I pushed up and away from him, still joined together, we watched each other.

When Parker smiled, the oddest sensation of wanting to cry washed over me. I held it together, never in my life crying during, or after, sex. But somehow he knew. Parker pulled me toward him, against his chest, and I lay there, listening to his heart.

When my breathing became normal, my cheeks no longer tingling, I lifted my head up.

"I know," he said, tucking errant strands of hair behind my hair. "I felt it too."

26

DELANEY

"Hey, stranger," Jules said on a break between customers.

Juliette and I met not long after she'd come to town in middle school with her mother. From Austin, they moved back to Cedar Falls where her grandparents had still lived at the time before they both passed. She was four years younger than me, so we didn't know each other well then but became friends when I moved back to Cedar Falls. Most of the girls I hung out with in high school moved out of town, and I considered Jules one of my closest friends.

Of course, us both being "artsy types" didn't hurt either. Although she was a writer, we often had discussions about the creative process, something a lot of people didn't really get, even though I thought most people had a creative side to them, whether they knew it or not.

"What are you doing in here?" I asked. "The festival is"—I waved a hand toward the door—"out there."

The Cedar Falls Winter Wonderland Festival was our town's way of getting people to the area during a typically slow time. Since I was working until three, for me it just meant a busier day than normal with foot traffic, which was fine. I never realized until taking this job how awful being bored was. I preferred busy any day.

"Just popping in to say hello. I'm meeting some friends soon for lunch. Apparently The Big Easy and Bella Luna are both jam-packed, so we may just head down to O'Malley's instead."

"Tell Beck I said hello. Pretty sure he's on for a double today."

With her jet-black hair and signature stacked jewelry, Juliette, or Jules as most people called her, always looked like she was ready for a rock concert. Not even a thick winter jacket and hat could hide her unique style. Jules definitely marched to the beat of her own drum, and I loved that about her.

"Will do. So"—she looked around the pharmacy—"where's he hiding? I know you don't go anywhere these days without him."

It was true. Parker and I had been together every day this week. Although he hadn't stayed the night since Tuesday, we'd done something each day. Even yesterday when he mentioned a guys' night with Mason and Beck, Parker had said, "We need to connect at some point," and we went to brunch before I started work.

"He's actually volunteering until two. Apparently Maggie roped him into manning the charity drive booth, although he didn't seem to mind all that much."

Maggie LeBlanc, the owner of a New Orleans-themed restaurant in the town square, was the chair of the event. It had been her idea a few years back, a way to liven up Cedar Falls in January.

"Volunteering. Of course. Is he really as nice as he seems?"

I asked myself that question at least once a day. "He really is.

I'll be honest, I thought for sure he was too good to be true. But he's genuinely an all-around great guy."

"No wonder Pia wanted you to get together with him sooner. Fucking Makis."

"Tell me about it. Part of me still feels like I'm walking on eggshells even though I know the two are like night and day."

Jules bit her lip. "Not to overstep, but you did ask me to remind you to listen to me the next time I gave you dating advice."

"I guess you're about to do that now?"

"I am. Let yourself love, Delaney. Forget Makis for good."

Loving Parker would be so easy to do. And hearing my ex's name reminded me of how little I'd thought about him recently. Every day that went by, the pain he'd caused by ending things the way he had ebbed further and further away.

"I'll consider it," I teased.

That seemed to be good enough for her. "In other news, I was talking to the owner of Cedarwood Grill the other day. My mom and I went in for lunch. He's doing some renovating on the dining room, and I may have thrown your name out for some commissioned artwork. Hope you have time in your schedule."

I appreciated that she'd thought to mention me. "I do. Any idea what he wants?"

"Not sure, but don't be surprised if he gets in touch."

"Thanks," I said as a customer came up behind her. "We need to catch up. Maybe next weekend? Parker's heading to Rochester for a building workshop."

"Sounds great. I've been dying to try that new winery on the south side of the lake. Maybe make a day of it?"

"I'm on early shift next Saturday, so maybe after that?"

"Perfect." Jules waved as she headed out. "See you later."

One customer turned into a fairly steady stream, and before I knew it, two hours had flown by. It was too bad I wasn't as excited about filling prescriptions as I was about painting for Cedarwood. I knew the vibe of the place and already had ideas. Of course, the owner might be going in an entirely different direction, but a few well-placed pieces could really liven up the place.

Not wanting to waste time heading home, I'd gotten ready for the festival that morning and slapped my lab coat over an outfit that would be covered anyway, winter jacket and all. Unfortunately, my replacement was more than twenty minutes late. All bundled up, I hurried to the town square where Parker was waiting.

He stood in front of the gazebo, which was decorated with blue and white lights for the festival, though it was hard to see them now. Later, at sundown, the entire square would come alive, the Festival Committee having put up almost as many lights in town as it did at the holidays.

Walking past the ice-carving demonstration, I tapped Parker on the shoulder from behind. Spinning around, he gave me a brief look before placing his gloved hands on my cheeks and kissing me, hard, on the lips.

I kissed back, not caring about the show we might be putting on.

"How was work?" he asked when we broke the kiss.

"Busy," I said. "Thankfully. How did the donations go?"

"Great. The boxes are overflowing with coats and hats and gloves."

"Awesome."

Parker took my hand. "Come on," he said. "We're late."

"Late for what?" I asked. As far as I knew, there weren't any timed activities or shows or anything.

"You'll see."

Walking past a hot cocoa stand at the edge of the square, Parker stopped and bought two of them. Giving me one, he took my hand again. We headed a half block down, past The Coffee Cabin and onto Mechanic Street where the cars had been moved to make way for one of the most popular attractions... horse-drawn carriages.

"Sorry," Parker said as we walked up to an older gentleman I didn't know. He was probably from the company that arranged the rides, didn't seem like a local. "All set."

Helping me up to the carriage, Parker sat, put a blanket onto my lap and pulled me into him as the driver asked if we were ready.

"You pre-arranged this?"

"I did. There was a massive line earlier, but I know one of the drivers. Not him," Parker clarified, nodding to ours. "I did some work on the other guy's house and pulled in a favor. Apparently they've been so busy they're packing them in."

I did notice there was room for at least four more people in our carriage.

"That was incredibly thoughtful," I said, warm and content. Snuggled into Parker's side, hot cocoa in hand, it was also incredibly romantic.

"Glad you like it."

We rode in companionable silence for a few blocks, spying festival activities which were centered in the town square but extending out to the side streets too. Almost every business was decorated in some way for this event.

"So how was your guys' night?"

I hated to admit it, but part of me wondered if he'd try to connect at the end of the night. I'd been surprised not to hear from him at all. Not even a good night text, something he'd begun to do after staying over Tuesday.

"Good. Nothing special. How was your night with Mom and Dad?"

"Uneventful. My dad is having back surgery in a few weeks, so that was the main topic of conversation."

"Is he alright?"

"Hopefully he will be after the surgery. He's had chronic back pain for as long as I can remember."

"That sucks. My brother Jimmy hurt his skiing one year in a bad fall. Flares up from time to time. Doesn't seem fun at all."

"So he's a skier too?"

"Yeah, both of my brothers are outdoor types, like me."

I looked over at him. Parker kissed me as the horse's hooves clanked from time to time when they hit patches of pavement not covered in snow.

"What is it?" he asked after we broke apart.

My eyes widened. How could he possibly know there was anything wrong?

"Nothing," I said, mostly meaning it. I was the one who had wanted to keep it casual. No way I would fess up to feeling a little off that he didn't text me last night. "I'm happy as a clam."

"Do you know what the full expression is?"

"What expression?"

"Happy as a clam."

Cedar Falls drifted by us as we talked. "I have no idea."

Parker finished his sip of cocoa. "It's… happy as a clam at high tide. Clams are harvested at low tide when they're exposed. At high tide, they're submerged underwater, all safe and sound."

"No kidding?"

"I'd never kid about something as important as a clam's safety. Now tell me what's wrong."

"Parker," I started. He shifted so we were face to face. "It's silly."

"Silly or not, I want to hear it."

"I'm serious. It's nothing—"

"And I'm serious. No lies between us. Ever."

He *was* serious, too. Somehow Parker could tell something was on my mind, and he wasn't going to let it go. "I just... got used to your good night texts." I added quickly, "See? I told you, it's nothing. So silly."

But he wasn't laughing. He was thinking. Probably wondering how to end this before it began after I just waved the "needy girl" flag in his face.

"If that's silly," he said finally, "then so is the fact that I picked up my phone and put it down a half dozen times, trying to decide if you'd welcome a good night text or if it was too much. I'm trying to be mindful of that first conversation in the Coffee Cabin. Things are moving quickly between us, and the last thing I want to do is scare you away."

"I'm trying to imagine you lying in bed," I admitted. "Actually debating that with yourself."

Everything Parker did was assured. He was the most quietly confident man I'd ever met. Not flashy, like Beck. But just someone who knew himself well.

"Forgive me if I only heard the first part of that. If you'd like, we can make it happen for real so you don't have to imagine it."

"You're a nut," I said.

"And you're getting a good night text every night now. I hope you know that."

"I hope you know I wouldn't mind. At all."

"And I hope you know... I don't want another Taco Tuesday."

That wasn't at all where I thought he was going with this conversation. "What do you mean?"

"I wanted to touch you all night. Kiss you the second you walked into the inn. But I'm trying not to push—"

"Push all you want," I said, the words flying from my mouth as I thought about Jules's advice.

"You sure about that?"

"Yes," I said, remembering how I'd felt just before falling asleep, wondering if maybe Parker had met someone and that was why he hadn't texted. Someone less fragile than me. "I don't want to be needy. That's not who I am."

Parker looked furious all of a sudden. "I swear to God, if I ever meet that asshole, I'm going to kick his ass for making you feel that way. Delaney," he said, "wanting to be reassured, knowing you care, isn't needy. It's hotter than hell. Please don't hold back. Not with me."

His words were like a soothing balm caressed over an open wound. One I thought had healed but that clearly still festered.

"I'm still waiting for the shoe to drop," I admitted. "No one can possibly be as nice, and understanding, and amazing in bed," I added with a smile, "as you. How haven't you been scooped up way before now?"

"Because I'm also damaged. My father—"

"Isn't you."

We pulled onto the block where our carriage ride would come to an end. I didn't want to get up. I wanted to stay here, in Parker's arms, talking, all night.

"To be clear," he said as the carriage slowed, "when we meet up with the others later, I'm not hiding anything."

"Good."

"We're together."

"We are," I agreed. To just to clarify. "As in..."

"As in, you are my girlfriend, Delaney. And I'm going to text you good morning, and good night, anytime we're not already together."

My pulse raced. This was really happening. "And seeing other people?"

The carriage stopped.

Parker slowly shook his head.

No.

Smiling, I tossed the blanket from my lap. "Well then. That was an eventful carriage ride."

Parker held my hand as I began to climb down. "Wait till you see what I have planned next, cupcake."

27

PARKER

"Look at him," I said as Beck made his way toward us.

Mason and I had been painting the hallway for an hour. With no guests, it was a good time to get it done, being the only indoor painting job left. At this point, every room of the inn had been renovated, and while there were a few bigger jobs remaining, most of those would wait until spring.

"He's a fucking mess," Mason said, more bluntly.

Since Beck and I were roommates, when I offered to move in to help Mason renovate, Beck immediately decided he would do the same. At the time, Mason had laughed at Beck's insistence he could be as useful as me, and it seemed like now he had a good reason to be skeptical. If he wasn't working, Beck was either screwing someone new, sleeping in... actually those were his three primary activities.

"I heard that."

Mason ignored him. "There's a pan for you over there."

Though slow to get going, when Beck did start painting, he got it done.

"I take it you had a good night?" I asked as we worked.

Though I'd stayed at Delaney's last night after the winter festival, having promised Mason we would paint today, I came back early and met Beck's "date" just as she was leaving.

"Eh. After you guys left it started to die down. Nothing special."

"And the woman I ran into on my way in this morning?"

Mason snickered.

When Beck didn't answer, I looked over at him. The poor guy seemed genuinely confused. "Seriously?" I asked. "You don't even remember?"

"Of course I remember," he said, leaning down to add paint to his roller. "Just can't recall her name at the moment."

Shaking my head, I didn't respond. Beck's choices were his own.

"I swear you're regressing," Mason said. As usual, he had less qualms than me about speaking his mind. Or pissing off Beck.

Maybe both.

"Maybe I am." Beck seemed less than bothered.

Since he was apparently in a good mood, despite Mason needling him, I pressed. "Talk to the parents lately?"

I didn't have to look at him to feel Beck glowering at me. "As a matter of fact, a few days ago. Same shit, different day."

I had a feeling.

When Beck went on a bender—staying out past closing, bringing more women home than usual—it usually meant he and his parents had had a falling out. Unlike my own rocky relationship with my father, Beck didn't discriminate between his parents. He didn't get along with either of them, for different reasons. He came from money. A lot of money. His dad was eternally pissed off Beck had no interest in taking over the family business, a bottling company that supplied most of the Finger Lakes wine bottles. His mother, though she'd never worked a day in her life, had even more to say about Beck's career choices. Or lack of them. Both divorced and remarried, his parents really were something else.

Which was why Beck had wasted a college degree to work as a bartender, not taking a dime from his parents... to piss them off.

"Mom? Dad?"

"Both. Fucking tag-team conference call. Mom was at Dad's office, estate planning or some stupid shit like that. Always a good time being lectured by them despite the fact that I'm thirty-one fucking years old."

"Good job, Parker," Mason said, refilling his pan with paint. "Just what we need. A hungover and jacked-up Beck."

"I'm not jacked up," he said, his tone saying otherwise.

I kept my mouth shut. If Beck wanted my advice, he'd ask for it. The guy didn't need another parent. He needed to figure shit out on his own.

"You and Delaney skipped out early from O'Malley's." Mason smartly changed the subject.

After the festival, we met a bunch of people, including Mason and Pia, at O'Malley's, but didn't stay long. "I met her after work, so we were out all day."

"Another sleepover too." Beck's voice had less of an edge, though he was still grumpy. I didn't take it personally.

"Probably not the last. We had 'the talk' yesterday."

"I heard about that," Mason said.

"Already?" I finished my section and moved down the hall.

"Last night. Apparently the girls chatted. Pia told me after you left."

"That was quick." Beck reached for the paint can at the same time I did. Letting him have it, I thought back to the carriage ride. To last night. To every day we'd spent together so far.

"Feels right," I said without much more to add. The guys would know. I never moved this fast.

"Not sure why we took the pact anyway," Beck mumbled, handing me the paint can.

I didn't respond since there wasn't much to say. He was right. But for some reason he seemed to give Mason a pass. Of the three of us, his parents' marriage wasn't fucked up. Just the opposite, but his dad did live with a broken heart when his mom died.

No one talked for a while, which gave me time to think. Time to imagine a scenario where things didn't work out between us, where Delaney and I split up but still saw each other through Mason and Pia.

Stop. There's no reason to think that way. Things are great between us.

My girlfriend. It had been a long time since I'd called anyone that, and even longer since I'd felt this way about a woman. This all-consuming need to be with her. Constantly thinking about Delaney when we weren't together.

It was fun. Exciting.

And scary as hell too.

28

DELANEY

I was meeting Jules and Pia at The Coffee Cabin for a little Sunday Funday brunch when I saw it. Stopping in front of the building a block off the square, I wondered how I hadn't noticed the sign before, unless it had just gone up.

The place was cursed.

It had been a toy store, a children's boutique and, most recently, a wine-tasting room. I thought that last one would stick. The place had been decorated to the nines, and the location was perfect for foot traffic. Sourcing from all local wineries, it borrowed from the concept of an urban tasting room but, in the end, that hadn't made it either. The "closed" sign went up a few weeks ago, the out-of-town owners who'd come to Cedar Falls on vacation and never left giving up their dream. They were a nice couple, retired, and had leased the small but cute building. Since she was an interior decorator, no expense had been spared to transform the decor to one of my new favorite places on the square to pop in for a glass of vino with the girls.

Now, it was for lease again. I heard the actual building was owned by Paul Baker. He owned The Coffee Cabin building and about five others around the square. He'd even tried to buy out Heritage Hill when Mason's father passed away unexpectedly.

Moving along, I headed to our pre-game meeting spot. Pia and Jules were already at a corner booth.

"I can't believe we've got you for the whole day," Jules said as I sat.

While it was true I had the day off completely and was thrilled, after breakfast, to hop around the wineries with the girls, I was also getting a bit antsy too. Parker left Friday morning for the three-day workshop in Rochester. He'd asked for me to come along, but there was no way I could get off both Friday and Saturday after taking the day for our ski trip.

"I'm excited," I said, sitting.

"We ordered you a coffee already," Pia said. "But nothing to eat."

"I'm feeling a chocolate croissant. For the sake of soaking up the wine, of course."

"Of course." Jules jumped up from her seat, heading to the counter. "We did the same. Great minds, and all."

"Sorry I was late. Did you know the Wine Barn building is available for lease? I stopped to take a peek."

"No, but I'm not surprised. That shut down a few weeks ago."

"One apple cinnamon muffin"—Jules put the muffin in front of Pia—"and a banana nut for me. They'll have your croissant in a second."

"Thanks. I'll get you at the winery."

"No worries." Jules got up again. "Be right back."

"I swear that building is cursed. Nothing has been in there for more than a few years, at most."

"What was it before the Wine Barn?" Pia asked.

She was so ingrained in Cedar Falls that I sometimes forgot Pia just moved here last year.

"It's been a hundred different things. It was a children's boutique last."

"The Wine Barn?" Jules put my croissant down.

"Yeah. Thanks." I pulled it toward me. "I was just telling Pia, the building is available for lease."

She looked up. Took a bite of her muffin. Stared at me.

"Um, am I missing something?" Pia asked.

"You should do it," Jules said to me before addressing Pia. "The last time it was for sale, Delaney considered leasing it for a hot second. To open up an art studio."

"Oh, wow." Pia turned to me. "I know you've mentioned it before, but I never thought you'd seriously consider leaving the pharmacy."

"Only because I spent years of my life and thousands of dollars in school to become a pharmacist. And an art studio probably would share the same fate as every other business in that building. Otherwise, I'd totally have considered it for real."

"I sense sarcasm." Jules's own voice was laced with it.

"Just a little." I took a bite of my croissant.

"All of that is true, but look at Mason. He couldn't be happier, and his entire life he wanted to be a cop."

"True," I said. "But I feel like you're a big part of that equation."

"Maybe," Pia agreed. "What about Parker? I really think he's serious about venturing out on his own. Something tells me this workshop will be the start of something big."

"I think it will too. He's really excited about it. But Parker spent four years earning a business degree that will be put to use if he does start his own home-building business. Mine, on the other hand, would be a big waste."

"That's one way to look at it. Another," Jules said, "is that learning never goes to waste. The universe works in mysterious ways, leading you to a path but waiting for you to take it. Sure, it's a complete one-eighty. But the biggest rewards in life come from the biggest leaps of faith. You'd talked about selling your own artwork and jewelry in the shop, using it as a warehouse base for an online business and running workshops, combining multiple income streams and not relying on foot traffic alone. I think it's a perfect plan."

Not wanting to insult her, I could say, "You would think so." Jules was very much like me. A creative type. An idea person. But taking so many math and science courses gave me another more practical side too.

"Maybe," I said, noncommittally.

"Why don't you let me help with some research on the viability of such a plan?" Pia asked.

If anyone had the resources to do just that, it was Pia. While her specialty lay in hospitality, turning around failing hotels and B&Bs was the reason Mason's father had hired her in the first place to manage Heritage Hill.

"I'd love that. But..." I didn't want to get ahead of myself; it was important to keep things real too. "We're just exploring. It's a huge step and, to be honest, it scares the crap out of me just thinking about it."

"I get it," Jules said. "I'm over here talking a good game but teaching classes and writing stupid articles just to avoid doing the big, hard, scary thing. I'll be the first to admit I'm a walking, talking 'do as I say and not as I do.'"

"We'll work on you next," Pia promised, winking at her.

This was why I loved my girlfriends. Lifting each other up with unquestionable support. "You guys are the best."

"And she's not even drinking yet," Jules teased. "Speaking of, where are we thinking to start? It might take a while to get a car in the off-season. Maybe I should put in for one now."

"No need." Pia finished up her coffee. "Mason is in town and will give us a ride to wherever we're going first. I told him he couldn't stay though. Girls' day and all."

"Awesome. I can't wait to get one or two in her"—she nodded to me—"and then ply her for dirt on Parker. She's been unusually tight-lipped about this one," Jules said to Pia.

"She has been," Pia agreed. "But thankfully I have all the inside dirt from Mason."

"Did Parker say something to him?" So much for playing it cool. Things were great with Parker. Beyond great, actually. Which was exactly why I was being tight-lipped. With Makis I'd gushed about how amazing he was only to have to turn around and tuck my tail between my legs so many times, not least when we broke up. Twice.

"Maybe a little." Pia smiled. "All good though."

I couldn't help it. Every part of me felt alive. I woke up earlier. Had more energy. Couldn't wait to get the day started to see him. Even something as small as a "Good morning" text made me smile for hours.

I hadn't wanted it at first.

Hadn't expected it so soon after Makis.

But there was no denying that I was falling in love with Parker Scott. Every time we were together I found something new to adore. His smile. His laugh. The little thoughtful things that made me wonder, still, if the guy was for real. It felt as if I could tell him anything. There were no judgments with him, ever.

And the sex.

Dear lord, Parker's dirty talking had only gotten dirtier. Filthy, really. And he could back it up.

"Alright. If you ladies are ready"—Pia crumpled her napkin and put it on the empty plate where her muffin had been—"who's ready for Sunday Funday?"

"Let's do this." Jules stood.

"Me," I said as my phone buzzed. I took it out from my jeans back pocket.

It was Parker.

29

PARKER

Hanging up with Beck, I called Delaney next. It rang twice before she answered just as I pulled onto the highway.

"Hey." Delaney's voice was like the first warm day of spring.

"Hey, yourself. I didn't expect to hear from you until later." I'd been planning to head straight to her house from Rochester.

"Slight change of plans. Have you talked to Mason yet?"

"Not yet. We're just leaving The Coffee Cabin now. Apparently he's going to be our chauffeur today."

"He'll tell you more but... do you mind if we meet at the inn instead of your house later?"

"Not at all. Is everything okay?"

"That depends on your definition of okay. I just got a call from Beck. He's... distraught."

She was clearly confused, but it was a long story. "Beck is distraught so we're meeting at the inn?"

"Basically. If you don't mind. He didn't say it outright, but I know him pretty well. I think he could use some company tonight. I already talked to Mason, and he said they'll be around later too, after your girls' day."

"Of course, that's not a problem at all. I'm glad the workshop went well. I'm excited to hear all about it."

We'd been texting all weekend, though this was the first we'd talked.

"I'm not sure how excited you'll be if I actually ran you through the details of log cabin building and marketing."

"I want to hear them either way. I'm jumping in Mason's truck now and will ask him what's going on."

"Sounds good. Later, cupcake."

"Bye, Parker."

The drive back seemed somehow longer than the drive to Rochester. If I thought before this weekend things were going well between us and that she was different than my past relationships, not seeing her for two and a half days solidified that fact.

Finally, after what felt like ten hours, I pulled into the inn and all but ran inside. As usual, everyone was gathered in the kitchen.

Not intending to be subtle about it, seeing Delaney casually standing there with a glass of wine in her hands, I walked straight up to her and kissed her like I'd imagined doing the whole way home.

Ignoring taunts like "get a room" and "enough already" from Beck and Mason, I stopped only when getting hard and being unable to walk to the fridge became a real possibility.

"Taste," she said, handing me the glass. "It's a new one from Golden Grove."

I took a sip. "Not bad," I said, whispering, "but I'd much rather taste you." Heading toward the fridge, I asked the group, "Where are we at?"

"Despite the fact that I don't need babysitters?" Beck said, his body language as he sat, slumped, on a kitchen island stool indicating otherwise. "We're all just really hungry. We waited for you to order Chinese."

"How's he doing?" I asked Mason, who handed me a bottle opener for my beer.

"Not good."

"Talk to me," I said to Beck, heading back toward Delaney. This might not be the reunion we'd hoped for, but I still got to be close to her. Leaning against the counter, like she was, I waited for my friend to open up.

The exact opposite of Mason, Beck had no problem sharing his feelings. Problem was, he had a lot of them. Sure, he was the life of the party, but the guy felt big. And I knew today was a bad day for him.

"I knew she was finished in April and maybe coming back. But I wasn't expecting it to be with some French asshole. Engaged. Fuck." He took a long swig of beer. Judging by the empties in front of him, it was one of many.

"Delaney, want to help me order?" Pia asked.

I was pretty sure two of them weren't needed to order Chinese food, but Delaney said, "Sure," as they headed out of the kitchen, presumably to leave the three of us to talk. I watched Delaney until she was gone and got caught by Mason staring at her ass.

Not caring, I focused back on Beck.

"You guys talk all the time. You're telling me this was a surprise?"

"I knew she was dating someone. But... engaged? Are you fucking kidding me?"

Beck had been in love with Mae O'Malley for as long as I'd known him. The two of them grew up next door from each other, and it still amazed me Beck—of all people—had never once made a move on her. Sure, she was a few years younger and by the time she was in high school Beck had been a freshman in college. But she hadn't left to attend a pastry school in France until a few years later.

Like Pia, Mae apparently saw through the show Beck put on for the rest of the world. He said once in college, drunk off his ass, that "Mae is the only person who really knows me." The next day, Cole had something to say about that since we were seniors by then, the four of us considering ourselves best friends who knew each other well.

But it was Mae we were talking about. The woman who required us to come up with the "never date your neighbor" rule when devising the bachelor pact. Because, in some alternate universe, if the very sweet Mae O'Malley ever realized her friend had a lifelong crush on her and, more remarkably, she decided to date Beck, it would be game over.

"You're telling me"—I tried to wrap my brain around it—"neither of her parents mentioned it? That they were so serious?"

Since Beck worked for her dad—O'Malley's was established by Mae's grandfather when Cedar Falls began to get developed—that seemed hard to believe. The mom worked there too, as the bookkeeper, though she'd been talking about retiring lately. Beck had a good relationship with the O'Malleys.

"I mean, I heard the guy's name before. What the hell kind of name is Mathieu, anyway?"

Mason was trying, and failing, to keep a straight face.

"It's the French version of Matthew," he said dryly.

Beck's phone buzzed. Looking at it like a lost puppy, he clicked a few buttons. Cole's voice came through.

"Hey, buddy. I'm sorry to hear about Mae."

"Sup, Cole?" I said.

"Hey, Cole," Mason greeted him.

"Thanks," Beck said. Apparently Cole just got the group text Beck had sent to us earlier.

"I guess we didn't need that rule after all." Beck hung his head. The guy had it bad. But that wasn't any surprise.

"Look at it this way," Cole said. "We took a pact for a reason. And yeah, Mason ended up being an exception. But how many of our parents ended up happily ever after?"

No one needed to answer that.

Zero.

As Beck and Cole talked, I thought of my own dad. On the outside, things appeared fine to everyone else. But as our family eroded from within thanks to his cheating and lies, not one of us got away unscathed. My brothers pretended it didn't affect them, but I knew better.

"Would it have been amazing to get together with Mae? Sure. At first. But they call it the honeymoon period for a reason. It doesn't last."

Mason and I looked at each other as Cole's "pep talk" seemed to be cheering up Beck. Not surprisingly, we couldn't give the same advice, given our positions. Mason was engaged. Delaney and I weren't there yet, but honestly, after this week-end, we seemed one step closer. It was true we hadn't been together long, but when you knew, you knew.

And I knew my feelings for Delaney were something different.

"Can you get a few days off? Come down to the city."

"I'm off next Friday," Beck said. "Maybe I can see about coming Thursday night. With the ski trip, it's probably all I can swing."

"I'll make sure it's worth the trip."

This had the makings of a shit show written all over it.

"Anyone else feeling an overnighter?" Cole asked through the phone.

"Pia and I are heading to Oregon next weekend to see her family. They're having some kind of engagement party or something."

"Oh, that's right," Cole said.

I was about to decline as well, but Beck's expression stopped me. He was like a ten-year-old boy who had just learned big eyes and a frown could make his mom say yes when the answer should be no.

"We'll see," I said instead, not intending to leave Delaney again so soon until Beck smiled so big, I had no choice but to reconsider.

"Come on, Park. Three of us. Like old times. Minus one."

"Look at you, doing math," I said, trying to avoid giving him an answer.

"Gotta run," Cole said through the phone. "Let me know either way."

"Will do." Beck clicked the phone to hang up after Mason and I said goodbye as if we wouldn't be texting him, probably later that night. Cole was the most bothered by group texts which, of course, meant we used any excuse to do it.

As if they'd timed it perfectly, Pia and Delaney came back just as Beck hung up with Mason.

"Did I hear Cole's voice?" Pia asked.

"Yep," Mason said. "Did you get me General Tso's chicken?"

"I did," she verified. "Beck, I think that's the first time you've smiled all night."

"Thank you, guys," he said. Beck didn't need to offer an explanation. We all knew what he was thanking us for.

"It's what friends do." I pulled Delaney toward me, and whispered just for her, "Later, I'll show you what boyfriends who miss their girlfriends do. Pretty sure you'll like it."

"Pretty sure I will," she said, settling into my side.

I would make sure of it.

30

DELANEY

"How long do you have? I want to show you something."

I was working second shift today, and since Parker's current job was in town, we agreed to meet for lunch at The Big Easy. They had a po' boy special on Tuesdays which was one of my favorites.

"I'll work late, so at least an hour. Maybe a little more. What's up?"

It was a cold one today, the temperature flirting with teens, but since I'd been meaning to show him and we were only a block away...

"How are you not wearing gloves?" I asked. Though he did have on a hat, his bare hands were making me feel cold as we walked.

"Why do you think I'm holding your hand?" he asked. "Forgot mine at the job."

His company was renovating a wing of the local middle school about ten minutes away.

"Sorry to drag you around town but I've been meaning to tell you all week. Look."

I pointed to the building, its "for lease" sign prominent in the window.

"For years I've imagined it as an art studio."

Parker let go of my hand, walked up the steps to the front porch, and peered inside. That he was taking it so seriously was only one of the reasons I loved him.

Loved him.

Admitting it to myself had been scary at first, but for the past few days, every time I looked at him, every time he texted or called, I knew it was true.

"Looks like a decent space," he said. "Can't say I've ever been inside."

"I have. There's a front showroom and the others have been converted to office space. I always imagined the front room being a place to have classes that you could see right through the window."

"Delaney—"

"Before we freeze to death, let's head to lunch while we talk."

Parker took my hand again. "Tell me more. What do you envision?"

I talked the whole way down the block. When we got to The Big Easy, the owner greeted us at the hostess stand. Even though Maggie was also the executive chef, she could be found front of house at least half the time. Everyone knew her and loved her.

"Y'all look like popsicles," she said, grabbing two menus.

"I still can't believe you left Louisiana for this weather," I said as she escorted us to a table. It was decorated to look like the inside of a New Orleans eatery, with a few more beads, Maggie admitted, than you'd usually find hanging around outside of Carnival season. The theming was fun, but what made The Big Easy a Cedar Falls staple was the food. And live jazz some nights of the week too.

"You'll do crazy things for family," she said. "Besides, we get back a lot. Here you go," she said as we took off our coats. "Drinks?"

"I'll have an iced tea, unsweetened, please."

"Sounds good. Same," Parker said as Maggie walked away.

"So anyway, I know it sounds nuts. But Pia is doing a little digging, market research and such. My parents would absolutely kill me if they even got a whiff of this but... I wanted to see what you thought."

Parker sat back in his seat, crossed his arms, and was quiet what felt like an hour. His opinion shouldn't matter so much, but I respected him, a lot. So it did matter. Especially since I couldn't talk to my parents yet. Normally with an important decision like this, I'd have already run it by them.

"Do you remember what you asked me when I tossed out the idea of a log cabin building business?"

I thought about it for a second. "I don't."

"You asked what was stopping me from starting my own company. So I'll ask you the same. Except, take your parents out of the equation. They love you and want to see you succeed, but the decision is yours. Not theirs."

I started to talk but he added, "And take college out too. Actually, everything that happened in the past, it's over. Looking forward and not back. What's stopping you?"

I thought about it as the waiter brought our drinks and handed us the menus, though I didn't need mine.

"Money," I said.

"There's business loans for that."

"And if it doesn't work?"

"You pay it back. It's just money."

"Just money." I laughed. "That little thing you need to live."

"You would manage, I'm certain. What else?"

"I'd be out of a job."

"Do you like your job?"

He knew the answer to that already. "No."

"So why would you want a job back you didn't like? This isn't a trial run, Delaney. We get one chance at it, and then we die."

The waiter had returned that very second. He looked at Parker strangely for a second before saying anything. "Best make it a good meal then. What'll you have?"

Parker and I both laughed at his quick comeback and ordered lunch.

"That was funny," I said of the waiter's timing and quick thinking.

"It was. But I'm serious. And yeah, Mason may have rubbed off on me. But he's seen so much shit that the whole 'memento mori' thing hits home for him in a real way. Which I get."

"Memento mori?"

"It literally means, 'remember you must die.'"

"Charming. I can see how that would be super motivational," I teased.

Parker smiled. "It's just a reminder of our mortality. A reminder to live."

"Sort of a macabre way of saying carpe diem?"

"Sort of, sure."

Memento mori.

"So are you saying I should go for it?" I asked finally, our po' boys coming already. The smell of roast beef and gravy reminded me that I was absolutely living life to the fullest at this very moment. Did it get any better than sharing good food with a person you loved?

"I'm saying, the decision is yours. And I support whatever decision you make, 100 percent."

That was so... Parker. I was about to tease him for not

answering completely but also thank him for being so amazing when my phone lit up. Normally I wouldn't have it on next to me at dinner, but my dad was heading to a pre-surgery appointment today, and I wanted to be sure he was okay.

I'm sorry. For everything. I miss you D.

I stopped chewing mid-bite. My heart thudded as I stared at the text from Makis. It was like being tossed in a time machine, the feeling of waiting for his texts, the hurt and pain, all bubbling to the surface.

What I would have given to get a text like that from him months ago...

"What is it?"

I looked up. Refusing to let myself start crying, I swallowed. Took a deep breath. How could he still have the ability to affect me this way?

"Makis."

Parker stopped chewing too. Rage, the kind I'd never expect from Parker, certainly had never seen from him before, danced in his eyes. Thank goodness Makis had only texted and hadn't actually come to Cedar Falls to say this in person. I really think Parker would have made good on his threat to pummel the guy.

He didn't ask what the text was about. Didn't chastise me for not blocking him which I totally should have done. At first I didn't have the heart, and these past few weeks, I hadn't cared enough to bother, never thinking I'd hear from him again.

"He says he's sorry. And misses me."

If our situations had been reversed, this was about the time I would ask Parker why his toxic ex was still alive and well in his phone.

"I should have blocked him. But I didn't want to at first, and then—"

"Delaney." Parker reached across the table and put his hand over mine. "You don't have to explain."

"But..." I tried to do just that.

"I'm serious. You don't. I just hate seeing you upset."

I put the phone down and wrapped my fingers through his. They were so different, and yet... hadn't Makis been like this at first? There wasn't a hint of the man that later all but ghosted me when I tried to get any clarification from him.

"I'm not upset," I said, shrugging off the thought. "At least, not anymore. It was just a shock to see his name pop up." I picked up the phone again. "Swipe. Delete."

Taking a bite of the sandwich, not even tasting it, I focused on the man sitting across from me. He didn't look as angry now. Just concerned.

Finished chewing, I reassured him. "Honestly, I'm fine. Eat up, you don't have a lot of time left."

He did, and eventually we moved on, talking about the building, Pia's research and just starting our own businesses in general. I knew very little about the legalities of it, how to even get started, but Parker did, business major and all.

It was a pleasant lunch and gave me a lot to think about, but Makis's text had taken away some of the joy that I'd been feeling just before he'd messaged. I hated him for that. For all of it. But I was even more angry with myself for letting any doubts about Parker creep into my head because of that asshole.

That was when my phone lit up again, but this time, it wasn't Makis.

31

"I'm getting married."

It wasn't at all what I expected my father to say. He'd texted earlier asking me to call him as soon as I got a minute. Stepping away from the construction area, I called right away. After Delaney's mother had contacted her at lunch the other day saying they'd discovered her father had high blood sugar when he went for his pre-surgery checkup, I wasn't taking any chances.

So no health crisis, but still concerning since my father didn't actually have a girlfriend.

"To who?"

It was a logical question, but the fact that I had to ask it was insane.

"Her name is Renee. Do you remember the woman I met in Cedar Falls?"

I resisted saying, "That would be hard to forget after I picked up your prescription for you." Delaney and I still got a good laugh out of that one.

"Yes," I said instead. "I do."

"We're going to Vegas this weekend. I know it sounds crazy, but she's the one. I'm sorry you won't get to meet her before the wedding, but at my age, you just can't dick around with these things."

There was so much to unpack, I didn't know where to start.

"Is she from Cedar Falls?" If nothing else, I could meet the woman before she jetted off to Vegas with my father. I hated to say it out loud to him, but Dad's business did extremely well, and this smelled suspiciously like a money grab to me.

"No, she was just passing through. She's from Geneva. And before you ask, because your brothers already grilled me, she's widowed and very financially independent as a loan officer. We'll have a prenup so no concerns there."

One piece of good news, I guessed.

I could have said, "Are you seriously marrying a woman you've known for a few weeks?" Or something like, "How do you know she's the one and you won't cheat on her left and right like you did with Mom?"

But trying to get through to my father was like talking to a brick wall. Been there, done that. It would end in an argument, and he'd be jetting off to Vegas either way. So there wasn't much point in giving an opinion he hadn't asked for.

"Congratulations, Dad," I said instead. "Have you told Mom?"

"I did last night." He paused. "Parker, I know I've been shitty to her. And to you guys, setting a poor example of a husband. But I've learned my lesson. And you'll like her. Maybe you can come home to meet her soon?"

His voice was so full of hope, there was no other response except, "Sure, Dad. We'll figure something out." Maybe I would take Delaney home to meet the family.

"Great. Thank you for being so supportive. I appreciate it. So what's new with you? How's Mason doing?"

"He still has some bad days, but mostly is doing good. Having Pia helps."

"I bet. And you?"

I could talk about Delaney, but something held me back. It had been years since I'd introduced a woman to my parents. I never wanted to get my mother's hopes up. She wanted desperately for us to get married.

Something my dad had said just hit me. "Did you say Renee is a loan officer?"

"I did. Why," he teased, "do you need a loan?"

"As a matter of fact, yes." I almost said "maybe" but thought of my advice to Delaney. If I was pushing her into fulfilling a dream, I could at least put my money where my mouth was. I probably knew the first day of the workshop, talking to some of the other guys in the business who agreed log cabin construction would be viable in my area, that I'd be doing this.

It was, as Mason said, "go time."

"I'm starting my own business," I said. "Log cabin home construction."

Letting that sit, wishing I didn't still care so much about my father's opinion, despite everything, I waited for his response.

Silence.

And then, "She'd tell you that you need a business plan and financial projections."

"Already working on it."

"Are there any others nearby Cedar Falls?"

I wasn't talking to my father anymore but a lifelong businessman. And a good one at that.

"No. The closest one is over two hundred miles away. We stayed in a place a few weeks ago at Crystal Peak, a colleague of

Cole's. I talked to the owner, and he said it cost him a pretty penny to bring in the builder from outside Syracuse."

"Have you compared the average build cost to incomes in the area?"

"Yes," I said, telling him what I already knew. It would be a viable business. The only one of its kind in all of the Finger Lakes. It was just a matter of securing a loan, finding guys and getting our first gig. "My biggest concern is finding the right team."

He agreed that would be a challenge, but "not one you can't overcome." We talked a few more minutes until he said, "Parker. I think you've got a winner on your hands."

We disagreed about a lot. And I'd never fully forgiven him for hurting my mom the way he had. But being honest, I said, "Thank you. That means a lot."

And it did.

This wasn't the way I'd planned to tell him. And I still hadn't wrapped my head around the whole shotgun wedding thing, but all in all, it was one of the better talks I'd had with him in a long time.

When we hung up, I stood there for a few more minutes.

My dad was getting remarried.

I was starting my own business.

Holy shit. This was really happening.

I needed to talk to Delaney.

32

DELANEY

"Can you grab me the plates?"

Parker brought the plates I'd set out earlier to me at the stove. Starting with the angel hair and then topping it with my mother's chicken française, I brought the empty pan to the sink while Parker carried our plates to the table.

It was the first time I'd cooked him a meal, and I wanted to make it perfect. Turning down the kitchen lights—I'd worry about the dishes later—I carried our glasses of wine to the small dining room I rarely used. With a view of the fireplace and a single candle set in the middle of the table, it was perfectly romantic.

We ate, talking about my dad's treatment for pre-diabetes and the fact that Parker now had a new stepmother he had never met. Yesterday we'd both met with the small business development center, Parker to have eyeballs on his business plan and me to learn about one in the first place. They'd also been able to verify that, yes, my building was still available just in case I wanted to move forward.

"The amount of work that it would require seems daunting," I said. "Yesterday I talked with the owner of a pottery studio in Seneca, and she was super helpful. Essentially, I would be starting two separate businesses, one retail and the other to offer classes. She suggested I start small with one product or focus. I love jewelry and painting equally, though, and have no idea which would be a better starting point."

"What about that jewelry shop in Skaneateles? Did you ever get in touch with them?"

"I did." Telling Parker all about our conversation, I watched as he finished his meal, sat back and listened intently to me. Having someone to bounce ideas off, especially someone going through the same process, was priceless.

"The big question," he said, standing up and taking our plates into the kitchen. "Have you talked to your parents yet?"

Coming back to the table and picking up his wine, Parker settled back in.

"No," I said. "With everything going on with my dad..." I shrugged. "I did talk to my brother, though. He was encouraging, as expected. I just don't want to go there until I'm certain about the whole thing. No point freaking them out if I change my mind."

Parker's brows raised. "Change your mind? As in, you've made the decision to go for it?"

That was the question of the hour. "Not completely. The thought of quitting my job is just..." How could I put it into words? Scary didn't quite do it justice. "Permanent. That job won't be there if the studio fails."

It wasn't the first time we'd talked about this, and I knew Parker's stance. He didn't say it outright, but he thought a lifetime was too long not to like your job. I agreed, on an emotional level, but every time I thought about all that schooling and how excited my mom had been that the position in Cedar Falls had opened up, it actually made me a little nauseous.

"Maybe writing your business plan and seeing what Pia comes up with in her research will help ease your mind. But," he cautioned, "at the end of the day, you'll have to get comfortable with the idea of risk too. There's never any guarantees when you're talking about starting your own business."

All true.

One thing that was guaranteed? I wanted to make this journey with Parker. Every day we spent together solidified the fact that we were perfect for each other. Not to say there wasn't a disagreement here and there. The other day we learned something valuable about each other. Namely, where Parker wanted to address and discuss any potential problems immediately, I tended to hold them in, take time to process first, and then address.

But at least we'd figured that out and agreed, though we had different styles of communication at times, the important thing was that eventually we talked it out.

"Keep looking at me like that, cupcake, and this dinner date is going to turn into an overnighter real quick."

"I'd be okay with that," I said, aware of the fact we'd just had a discussion about maintaining our own spaces for now. This was still very new, and neither of us wanted to jump into essentially living together after just a few weeks.

On the other hand, nights we spent alone sucked. I thought about him sleeping alone in a bed just a few minutes away at Heritage Hill and, more than once, had to stop myself from getting in my car and showing up on the inn's doorstep.

"Yeah?"

He stood up.

Dressed in jeans and a button down, sleeves rolled, knowing how much I loved that, Parker made his way over to me. Spinning my chair around, he squatted down in front of me. Never knowing what he was up to, my heart began to race.

Parker knew I was anticipating something. His slow smile told me it would be good too.

"What did I tell you about wearing leggings?" he asked, running his hand up my calf.

I swallowed. "That I should only wear them if I didn't care whether or not you ripped them off my body. Or something like that."

He chuckled. "Yeah. Something like that."

Parker pulled my legs open. As he did, my phone buzzed. "Check," he said. "Make sure Dad's okay."

I loved him. There was zero doubt about it. I absolutely had fallen in love with this man, and I just had to find the right time to tell him. Or wait for him to say it first. I still wasn't sure which.

Reaching over to the table, I grabbed it, just to be sure my father was fine, and brought it down to my lap to see.

Parker and I both stared at the name that popped up in a text.

Makis.

He stood up.

I closed my legs and clicked on the message.

Please talk to me. I miss you D.

Looking up, I wished I hadn't. Parker was pissed.

"I thought you were blocking him after his last text."

I tossed the phone onto the table and stood too. "I never

texted him back," I said. "And then didn't think of it again. His number got buried—"

"Delaney," Parker said in a tone that was unusual for him. "You can't tell me you forgot completely. That your ex-boyfriend, the one that crushed your spirit, comes back from the dead, and you don't think about it for a second? Enough to remember to block his number?"

I didn't answer. It wasn't that I was trying to lie to him, but I didn't want Parker to think there was anything there. My feelings for Makis were dead and buried.

"Maybe for a second," I admitted. "But I'm just not that kind of person. I've never unfriended or blocked someone in my life. It feels almost mean. But that doesn't—"

"Mean? You didn't want to be *mean* to the guy that treated you like absolute shit? Come on, Delaney. You can do better than that."

He'd walked into the living room, and something stopped me from following him. Parker wasn't being himself, and there wasn't much more for me to say. I didn't block him. But I should have. And here we were. Maybe it made no sense to Parker, but that was the truth. "There's nothing there," I said quietly. "I should have blocked him," I admitted.

Waiting for Parker to accept my words, knowing he would because that was the guy he was, I headed to the kitchen in the meantime. Started doing the dishes. Remembering the conversation we'd just had about disagreements. Parker liked to talk things out. Not let them "stew." I would block Makis's ass in front of him, explain once more there really wasn't anything there and...

No. Better yet, I'd be even more honest. I would tell Parker how I really felt about him. How could I possibly care a lick about Makis when I was deeply, head over heels in love with Parker?

Turning off the water, I dried my hands, hoping it was enough time for Parker to cool off, and headed into the living room.

But I couldn't tell Parker I loved him. Because he was gone.

Parker

33

PARKER

The second I walked into O'Malley's, I wanted to turn around and go back. If Beck hadn't spotted me and called me over to the bar, I would have. Instead, I walked the distance from the door of our trusted corner pub to my friend and sat on a stool.

Before I said a word, a cold beer was in my hand.

"On the house." I wasn't sure how Beck knew, but he did. "Be right back," he said, heading over to another customer. There weren't many of them on a twenty-degree Wednesday night. Thankfully.

"What's up?"

I looked from the bottle to my friend as Beck waited. After that night in the kitchen, none of us had uttered Mae's name. No one said a word. But I could tell Beck was still not himself, and maybe that was how he knew I wasn't myself either.

"Delaney."

If I said any more, I'd sound like some pathetic asshole. "She didn't block her ex." Since when was I the jealous type? Especially of a guy like that. But when I saw his name on Delaney's phone, I hadn't been able to think straight.

"That's not a lot to go on," Beck said finally.

"I know."

It probably wasn't the answer he'd been expecting. But it was the only one I had.

"Give me a minute." Beck headed to the opposite end of the bar to fill a drink order for the waitress.

In the meantime, I stared at my bottle, waffling between sending Delaney a text, apologizing for leaving, abandoning my beer and heading back to her house, and my current course of action—to sit here and do nothing.

Turns out, I went with option three.

"Hey," a gruff voice from behind said.

Mason sat on the stool next to me.

"What are you doing here?" I knew for a fact he and Pia were supposed to be at dinner. They'd asked us to go along, Delaney being off tonight, but we'd already planned for a solo night at her house.

"I dropped Pia off and came over."

Since it was all he said, Mason not a man of many words, I took a guess at how that had happened.

"Beck texted you?"

"I did." Beck slid Mason's drink to him.

"I was just pulling into the inn," Mason said. "Pia was tired and told me to come solo."

"You didn't have to come at all," I said. "Everything is fine."

"Oh, yeah? Doesn't look fine." Mason took a swig of beer.

I closed my eyes. Tried to block everything out, but that didn't make the vision go away. My mother's head was down, at the kitchen table. She was crying so hard, I'd turned and walked away. Seeing her like that had been a shock. Of course my mother had cried before. She did it a lot, actually. Sad movies. While reading books. My mother was as sentimental as they got. But I'd never, ever, heard her cry like that.

I waited in my bedroom for her to come and explain. Tell me who died. Or was sick. But she never came, and I'd been too afraid to ask what was going on. It wasn't until she came to tuck me in, hours later, that I asked her what was wrong.

"Nothing for you to worry about," she'd said. Too young to press her on it, I accepted Mom's words and went to bed. It was more than six months later that I'd pieced two and two together when my brother overheard an argument between my parents.

My mother had cried alone at the kitchen table because she found out my dad had cheated. It was the first, but not the last, time.

The worst part? I confronted my father, though not at first. I could remember his words to this day.

It just... happened. No one sets out to cheat on their wife. I loved your mother. Wouldn't have married her otherwise. But even the strongest of us has a weak spot. Who knew mine would be fidelity?

It never made sense to me. How could something like that just... happen? And if he hadn't intended it, loved my mother like he'd said, could anybody find themselves in a similar circumstance?

Me?

Delaney?

"You look like shit," Mason said.

"Thanks."

"It's bad," he said to Beck.

"I know. That's why I told you to come. Parker," he said to me. "This isn't you. What's up?"

I wanted to confide in my friends. Not long ago, we did the same when Beck found out the love of his life was getting married. And when Mason and Pia hit a rocky patch before he decided to quit the force and take over the inn, the normally stoic former Army Ranger talked to me about it. There was no reason for me not to do the same.

But I couldn't.

"Maybe I shouldn't have stayed the night." I saw Mason and Beck exchange a look. It didn't matter. What was done was done. Next steps were mine alone to take.

"I don't know what's going on," Mason said. "But I do know what Pia tells me about how Delaney feels about you."

"How she feels about me now," I clarified. "There's no doubt she likes me, but is that enough?"

"Pretty sure her feelings are stronger than that," Mason said. "As to your question. You know as well as I do, there's no future. No past. Just the present."

He was right. The guys were no fortune tellers.

"You still going to Cole's tomorrow?" I asked Beck.

"Yeah. You thinking of coming?"

"If you can wait until lunch. I'll head into work early and finish up by then. Friday shouldn't be a problem since the school is having some special event so we can't get in there. Working the weekend instead."

"Sounds good to me." Beck was clearly thrilled to have the company.

He walked away, to a customer. Mason and I didn't say anything for a while.

"Just do yourself a favor, buddy," Mason said finally. "Don't make the same mistake I did with Pia."

"What's that?"

"Letting the past haunt me. Almost fucked things up for good. You know it as well as anyone."

And that was it. We didn't talk about Delaney for the rest of the night.

But I did text her.

> I shouldn't have left. It wasn't about the text. It was about me. I grew up believing love meant betrayal, and when I saw that message, I panicked. Truth is, I don't want to be that guy. I want to trust this. Trust you. If you'll let me.

She never responded.

* * *

Driving into Manhattan was also a real joy. By the time we found a spot on Cole's street, it was well past four. Dropping our bags off in his apartment, we were in The Midnight Owl by four thirty.

I'd been here a few times before. It was quintessential Cole.

"Do you need an IQ over one-twenty to get into this place?" Beck asked as we walked inside. Vintage decor, dim lights and more tweed than probably in all of Greenwich Village, it had a definite vibe.

"One-thirty," Cole said dryly.

"So, like, 2 percent of the population? Doesn't seem like a sustainable business model."

I looked at Cole. He nodded and shrugged.

It was something we did often, silently verifying a Beck-fact that seemed too specific to be right, but usually... it was. The guy really did hide his intelligence well. Most of the time.

We were there less than an hour when Cole introduced us to the guy with the log cabin. I swiveled around on my stool, and he declined my seat but said he wanted to thank me for meeting with the contractor.

"It was no problem at all," I said. "Did you get them to fix it?"

"I did," Cole's professor friend said. "And Cole tells me you might be getting into the log cabin construction business?"

"I'm working on a loan now," I said, leaving out the part about waiting for my new stepmother to get acclimated to her new job. I wondered what her adult children thought of her up and moving, after getting married, of course, to a new town.

"Good for you. I have the name of the guy who did mine if you want it? I'm sure he'd talk to you. Really nice fellow. He took over for his father who recently retired. They did a great job, I think. But what do I know about home building?"

"They definitely did a good job. I'd love the contact, if you don't mind."

"Not at all."

When I pulled out my phone to put his number in there, a familiar name filled my screen. Swiping up, I cleared Delaney's text for now and exchanged information with him. We chatted for a few more minutes before he moved on.

"Cole," I said, standing and handing him my credit card. "Get him a drink, and another round for us. I'll be right back."

Before he could refuse it, I shoved my card into his hand and walked away, through the crowd and out the front door. It was freezing as hell, but I couldn't hear for shit in there. Hitting a few buttons, I waited.

She picked up immediately.

"Hey."

The bar door opened. I stepped off to the side.

"Hey."

Closing my eyes, I could picture her. Delaney in the hot tub. Delaney in our bedroom in the log cabin. Scene after scene played through my mind like a mini-movie of our short but fun-filled courtship.

"Glad you called."

"I just saw your text," I said.

"I got yours from last night."

She sounded sad. Defeated. The opposite of the Delaney I knew.

"I wasn't sure you got it," I said.

"Honestly, I didn't know exactly how to respond. I appreciate that you opened up and can understand why you panicked. But I can't take it back, not blocking him. And don't have any other reason for it except the one I gave you."

I believed her. "I know."

"Do you?"

"Yes, I do."

She sighed. "I wish you hadn't left."

So did I. "Do you remember what we talked about, in the beginning?"

"We're just two not-terrible-looking people, afraid of commitment, who like cupcakes. That part?"

"Yeah." I smiled, despite how shitty this felt. "That part."

"Of course I do. But I also remember the guy in the horse-drawn carriage who asked me to be his girlfriend." She sighed. "But this doesn't feel like a Cinderella story."

"We never did look back. Maybe the carriage did turn into a pumpkin and we didn't see it."

"And maybe we'll get a happily ever after too."

I hoped so. "I don't want to hurt you, Delaney. That's the last thing I want."

"I know," she said, echoing my words. "Where are you guys?"

"A place called The Midnight Owl. A bar full of Cole-types."

"Sounds like fun." I could hear the smile in her voice, which made me feel a little bit better.

"That's yet to be determined."

"Go ahead," she said. "Have fun with Cole. After I didn't get back to you, I just… wanted to explain. Or at least tell you that I wasn't playing games or trying to stonewall you. I just didn't know what to say to make it right."

I knew the feeling. "I hear you," I said. "Talk when I get back?"

"I'm staying at my parents' tomorrow night."

"Oh, that's right, the surgery is tomorrow. Text me and let me know how it goes."

"Will do."

"Alright. Talk soon."

Cupcake.

I left that part unsaid.

"Bye, Parker."

Hanging up, I looked at my phone, hoping I wasn't too late to fix this.

34

DELANEY

With terms like laminectomy and bony arch of the vertebra running through my brain, I found myself on a detour on the way to work. Having left early to walk by the now-closed wine-tasting room once again, a now-daily ritual, it was almost as if my feet moved of their own accord toward The Coffee Cabin.

Dad was going to be fine, but seeing him in the hospital yesterday, so fragile and vulnerable looking, had been jarring. Of course I knew my parents wouldn't be with me forever, but so often I was able to push aside any thoughts of a world without them. Between Mason losing his dad and my own having complications on what should have been a standard pre-surgery checkup, thoughts of something bad happening to them persisted.

Between that and what was happening with Parker, pulling myself out of bed this morning had been more difficult than usual. Looking at my phone, not seeing Parker's name pop up, had been disheartening, if expected. I might not have panicked except for our talk just a few days ago. Knowing he liked to work out problems immediately, rather than sitting on them, meant the guy was genuinely confused about moving forward.

Opening the door to the coffee shop, I resisted second breakfast, having already eaten a scrambled egg and piece of toast at home, but the smell of fresh baked goods got to me. Considering it a win when I only ordered a coffee, I took a deep breath and said, "Is Paul around, by chance?"

"He's in the back." The young college girl who I'd only seen working a few times before seemed unsure about what to do next.

"Can you tell him Delaney Thorton would like a brief word with him?"

"Uh, sure."

What the hell was I doing?

Maybe it was the lack of sleep after talking to Parker. More likely it was seeing my dad in that hospital bed with Parker's words ringing in my ears.

This isn't a trial run, Delaney. We get one chance at it, and then we die.

"Morning, Delaney," Paul Baker said, coming out from the back.

He was about my father's age, maybe a few years older. He was a regular at the pharmacy. Paul believed in frequenting locally owned businesses and wouldn't be caught dead ordering from a chain of any sort, pharmaceuticals included.

"Good morning," I said as he indicated a seat in the corner.

"What can I do for you?"

Ohmygod, ohmygod, ohmygod. What the hell was I doing?

"Well," I hedged before willing myself to just spit it out. "I wondered about the wine bar building. I've noticed it's for lease?"

Paul sat back in the corner booth. "Yeah, unfortunately. I

thought they had a winner, working with local wineries, Emilio... Urban wine-tasting rooms are popping up all over the place. It's too bad, really."

"Do you think there's a reason that particular building has had a difficult time maintaining businesses? I know it's a block off the square, but a lot of successful businesses are without a problem."

He seemed confused why I'd ask the question, but Paul was too polite not to answer. "I don't think it's the location, to be honest. We have a sign on the corner pointing down the street to foot traffic. And the children's boutique actually did well. They closed for personal reasons."

"Oh, really?" I hadn't known that.

"Why do you ask?"

Here went nothing.

"I've actually been eyeing that place up for a long time," I said, aware that I wasn't doing myself any favors letting him know how much I wanted that particular place. Maybe I wasn't a true businesswoman at heart, but if I was going to do this thing, I'd do it my way. And if being honest shot me in the foot, so be it. "You know I make and sell jewelry—"

He smiled. "And art." Paul nodded to one of my earlier pieces. It was a simple object watercolor but fit perfectly with the decor. Paul bought it at a craft fair in the square one summer when I had a table there.

"And art," I agreed. "For years I considered opening a studio, a place to sell my own pieces but also offer classes. I'm passable at pottery too and could have jewelry making, art, pottery... but actually," I said, knowing I was talking fast, "in my business plan, I'm starting with the retail and adding classes later. I've done some research"—actually Pia did more of it, and so far seemed to think the studio would be viable—"and have worked with the small business center a bit since this isn't my forte. Anyway, I wondered if the building is still for lease and if you could give me the costs?"

Paul was quiet for a second, likely taking it all in. Leaning forward, he broke out into a very encouraging smile. "Delaney," he said. "I think that would be an excellent asset to the town. You are obviously very talented and have thought the business through. I love it."

I love it.

He was also a businessman looking to lease the building. The practical side of me tried not to get too excited. "I know it's not your job to predict the feasibility of having a profitable business but—"

"It's a great idea. I wouldn't bullshit you, Delaney. Your father would have my head on a platter otherwise."

My father was a big guy, but, in truth, he was a teddy bear too. "I haven't spoken with my parents yet, so if I could ask for your discretion on this." I swallowed. "I did earn a degree and have a job which, obviously, I would have to forfeit to move forward."

"I understand. It's a scary thing, especially having a lot of time and money invested in your current career." He grinned. "I have a degree in forestry. Wanted to work in forest conservation, if you can imagine that. Never even had a job in the industry."

"Forestry?"

"It's a long, convoluted story. Point being, I understand your struggle. As for the cost, it's fifteen dollars a square foot, so fifteen thousand a year. That includes utilities, and there's no pass-through clause for taxes, but you are responsible for building upkeep and any necessary maintenance or repairs, including landscaping. You'll also need your own insurance as well."

I didn't have a clue what the tax stuff meant, but the cost was actually lower than expected with utilities included. As for repairs... Nope. I would not think of Parker at the moment.

"That's great to know," I said. "As I gather information, would it be possible to let me know if anyone else is interested in the building? As you can imagine, there are a lot of moving parts here."

Paul looked up, waved a hand, and focused back on me. "I have a meeting, but come by anytime with additional questions. The building is yours if you want it. You'll have first crack at it if anyone else is interested, but as of this moment, you're the first to inquire. So take your time, get your ducks in a row and stay in touch."

I stood, not wanting to hold him up. Reaching out my hand, I shook his. "That is incredibly gracious, Paul. I can't thank you enough."

"My pleasure. I hope it works out. A studio like yours, as I said, would be a great asset to downtown Cedar Falls. Let me know if you need anything at all."

"Thank you again," I said as he moved off.

Sitting back down, not surprised the coffee shook a bit in my hand, I digested everything he'd said. At least I didn't have to worry about dragging my feet and having someone scoop the building out from under me.

My phone buzzed. I took it out. Not Parker but my mother.

I clicked the text, any joy at the meeting with Paul instantly vanishing.

Call me ASAP.

35

PARKER

Delaney hadn't texted yet.

She'd be finished with work by now and was likely already at her parents' where she planned to stay for the weekend. Despite that she was supposed to have called to let me know how the surgery went, so far, nothing.

"Sorry we had to come back," Beck said, pulling into Heritage Hill. "Friday night in the city would've been a good time."

A few weeks ago? Sure. Tonight all I wanted to do was be with Delaney.

"Hey. You alright? You never did say what happened the other night."

Ah, fuck it. If there was anyone on the planet less judgmental than Beck, I didn't know them. "Her ex texted at lunch one day, saying he was sorry and all that." We continued to talk as Beck parked and the two of us walked inside. "Delaney said she should have blocked him but hadn't. And would. The other night, he texted again as we were... ah, finishing dinner."

"What did he say?"

"The usual bullshit. I'm sorry and all that."

"So she never blocked him?"

We headed inside. There were lights on at the inn, but the house portion was dark. Mason and Pia must have been out. Hanging up our coats and tossing our bags to the side, we headed, as usual, to the kitchen.

"Beer?"

"I have time for one," Beck said, sitting at the island.

Grabbing us each a bottle, I pulled off the caps and sat across from him.

"No. She never blocked him."

"Why?"

"Said it wasn't in her nature. Honestly, I left and never heard her out, so we didn't talk about it until the next day."

"That doesn't sound like you." I was about to agree, when Beck said, "Actually, come to think of it, you do that with your dad a lot."

"Yeah because arguing with him is pointless. I've never met a man so impervious to advice. From anyone. He's as thickheaded as they come."

"Mine would give him a run for his money in that department." Beck shook his head. "I dunno. Who am I to say anything when it comes to women?"

I didn't answer.

Beck waited.

"I assumed that was a rhetorical question."

Swinging down the rest of his beer—Beck was a record-holder among the four of us for quick drinking—he stood up. "It was, I guess. Talk to Mason. Or even Pia. They might be able to help."

"Thanks." I laughed. That was useful.

"I do like her, though. Delaney."

Beck tossed his empty bottle into the recycling bin, slapped my shoulder and said, "Come down to the bar later."

"I might."

I do like her, though.

I liked her too. But apparently she didn't feel the same. I looked at my phone. Still nothing. I tapped a button on my phone and a familiar voice came through. I put her on speaker.

"Hi, sweetheart."

"Hey, Mom."

"What's wrong?"

I smiled. That was so like her. "Nothing's wrong."

"Calling on a Friday night? Something's wrong," she countered.

"Just a thing with a girl I've been dating."

Silence. And then, "I can count on one hand how often you called me for advice about a girl."

"Not true. We talked about it all the time."

"In middle school. Maybe high school. But not in a long time."

"Only because I haven't had many serious girlfriends since."

"So it's serious?" My mother didn't even bother hiding her surprise or hopefulness.

I told her everything. From the ski weekend up until this past week. Waiting for her response, I felt as stupid as I had admitting to Beck I'd basically lost it over an ex.

"I can see why that upset you," she said.

"You can?"

"Of course. You went through the wringer with your father. I'm sorry about that."

Was she kidding me? "Mom, you have nothing to be sorry for. Dad was a complete asshole. Sorry for my French. Why would you apologize for him?"

"I'm not apologizing for him, sweetheart. I'm just sorry it happened and tainted your view of marriage. I know about your pact with the boys."

I'd been about to take a drink, but at that, my hand froze mid-air.

"Excuse me?"

"Beck told me once. You guys were here, visiting, and I think he had a bit too much to drink that night. I asked if you had any serious girlfriends and he told me about it. I doubt he even remembers. Poor kid was drunk as a skunk."

I remembered that night, wanting to go back home sooner, knowing my mother would be waiting up for us. It was a year or so after college, and Cole had come too. The four of us together always spelled trouble.

"Mom," I asked, suspicious. "Did you ask Beck that because he was drunk? Thinking to fish information out of him."

"Of course I did," she said unabashedly.

Laughing, I was about to tease her when Mom cut me off. "Point is, you'd never have taken such a pact if things worked out between your father and me. But like your friends, it just happens to be a bad example. There are plenty of good ones too. Look at your Aunt Cathy and Uncle Dave. Or Mason and Pia. Or your dad and his new wife." Mom laughed at her own joke. She really was a piece of work.

"I know," I said. "And Delaney really is something special. She's cute and perky, but sexy and smart too. Always has a smile on her face."

"Sounds like someone I know."

Me.

We really were good together, Delaney and me.

"I'd love for you to meet her," I said, answering my own unasked question about the state of our relationship.

"I'd love to meet her too."

"Oh hey, Mom, speak of the devil. She's calling now."

"Go ahead. I'll talk to you later. And tell the girl you love her. Bye, sweetie."

As I switched over, it took a second for my mother's words to sink in.

Tell the girl you love her.

I did. And here I was telling Delaney to live in the present, not the past, or future. Time for me to do the same.

"Parker?"

I could tell immediately something was wrong.

"What is it?"

"Are you back in town?"

She was scaring me. "I am. Delaney? What's wrong?"

"Good. Can you come to the hospital? We're in room 2604."

"Your dad?" I asked. It took me a second to remember he'd had the surgery that morning and that Delaney was fine.

"Yeah. There's been a complication."

Fuck. I headed to the door.

"I'm on my way."

36

DELANEY

"He's here," my mother said from the door. She'd gone to the nurse's station to ask them a question and apparently found Parker along the way.

Dad was sleeping, finally. It was my mother, after I'd told her all about what was happening with Parker and me, who said I should tell him to come.

"Texting is so impersonal," she said. "Talk to him in person."

Since I refused to leave the hospital, I asked him to come. Heading into the hallway, I made the strangest introduction ever.

"Mom," I said, "this is Parker." And since I had no idea where we stood at the moment, I left out, "my boyfriend." "Parker, this is my mother."

"I'm pleased to meet you, Mrs. Thorton, and am sorry it's not under better circumstances."

"Thank you, Parker," my mother said.

He looked at me. "He'll be alright," I said. "But there were some complications with the anesthesia. He had some difficulty breathing after it wore off. Apparently there's a mucus buildup in his lungs, a rare side effect, and they are keeping him to watch for any signs of a lung collapse."

"But he's going to be okay?"

"God willing," my mother said.

I tried not to roll my eyes, remembering my mother had been through a scare today. "The doctor said he will be fine, but they just want to get his breathing under control before letting him go. There's a lounge," I said, then to my mom, "I'll be back in a bit."

"You don't have to stay," she said. "He'll probably stay sleeping for the night."

"I know. I'll leave at ten."

"It was nice to meet you, Parker," she said as I guided him down the hall toward the family lounge area. With luck, everyone would be gone by now.

"Why ten?" he asked as we walked.

"Because that's when they'll kick me out."

Thankfully, the lounge was empty.

The second we walked inside, Parker pulled me into him. Slammed against his chest, engulfed by his arms, I didn't know what to say. So, of course, I cried.

I cried to be in his arms after wondering if it would ever happen again.

I cried because my dad would be okay, and because for a little bit this morning, I hadn't been certain.

I cried because the meeting with Paul left me more certain, but scared, about my decision.

He held me, saying nothing. When I finally picked my head up, thankful Parker wore a sweater that had soaked up most of my tears, words failed me.

Turns out, I didn't need them.

Bending his head down, Parker's lips found mine. He kissed

me so tenderly that for a second I thought maybe it was a parting kiss. A goodbye.

Breaking the kiss too soon, he stood back.

Grasped my cheeks in his hands.

"I love you, Delaney."

His words sank in. And when they did, I could only think of one thing to say. "I love you too, Parker."

This second kiss was more demanding, one that could easily spiral out of control had we not been in the visitors' lounge of a hospital. A beeping from the nurse's station reminded us of the fact. Pulling away, I looked up at him.

"Where is your jacket? It's like ten degrees out there?"

"Seventeen," he clarified. "I didn't stop to put one on when you called."

"I'm sorry if I scared you. I just... wanted you here."

"I'm glad you called," he said. "And I am so sorry for having left that night. I just..."

"You don't have to explain. The important thing is that you're here now."

"And I am not going anywhere, if you'll still have me?"

"Are you kidding? The last few days have been miserable without you. I wanted to tell you that night, wanted to say that I loved you, but"—I stopped, unwittingly reminding him of why we'd never finished our conversation—"I get why you left."

"Come here."

Parker pulled me back into his chest, and I stayed there for another few minutes. Would never have moved if my mom hadn't come to find us.

"Your dad is awake. I thought maybe you'd want to introduce him to your boyfriend?"

I looked up at Parker, who smiled at me. It was all the confirmation I needed. He was still my boyfriend, and I his girlfriend, except we were even more committed to each other tonight. Those words, "I love you," had never meant more coming from a man, mostly because I knew they were true. Him being here, without a jacket... the look in his eyes... saying it had only sealed the deal. He loved me, and I loved him.

"So much for us being two people, afraid of commitment, who like cupcakes," I whispered as we followed my mom back to my dad's room.

"Speaking of, I got some for you at a place near Cole's that's supposed to be famous for them."

"Oooh, now I'm excited."

"Good," he said. "That's what I was going for." Not expecting him to slap my ass, I started laughing as the nurse caught him and smiled. Parker pulled his hand back and smoothed out his hair just in time as my mother looked back at us.

Suddenly, he was the picture of innocence, smiling at my mother as if he were a damn altar boy.

"Oooh, you are wicked," I whispered to him.

"Just wait until you see what I do with one of those cupcakes you're excited about, and you'll know the meaning of the word."

"Is it ten o'clock yet?"

Parker barked out a laugh just as we headed into my dad's room.

37

PARKER

What a day.

Everything that could have gone wrong on the job did. The only bright spot was being able to see Delaney for dinner, but she'd been called into work. We agreed to meet at O'Malley's when she got off, so in the meantime I made myself useful around the inn, which was where I noticed a crack in one of the bathroom walls on the inn side of the building. Hoping it didn't lead to bigger issues, I inspected it with a putty knife to see if it was just superficial. Unfortunately, it didn't seem to be. My guess was moisture infiltration, which wasn't going to make Mason very happy.

By the time I'd taken a shower and headed down the street, I was tired and starving. Wishing Delaney wasn't working until nine, I almost headed to the pharmacy instead, but having skipped lunch, I probably wouldn't be the best of company. Instead, I headed inside, surprised by how busy it was for a Thursday.

"Hey, cranky pants."

Not in the mood for Beck's antics, I sat down. "I didn't say a word."

"You have that look about you."

"Beck, can I talk to you for a second?"

"Hi, Mr. O'Malley," I said to Beck's boss. He was a big guy who often said he spent too many years eating wings and not enough eating celery instead.

"Sure." Beck slid me a beer and headed to the side of the bar. Watching Mr. O'Malley, I wondered what they could be talking about. He didn't usually work late, the owner and his wife typically leaving late shifts to Beck and the bar's other manager.

"What's wrong?" Beck looked like he was ready to murder someone when he came back. "Beck?"

"Nothing."

"Now who's the cranky pants?" I said, throwing the ridiculous moniker back at him. "What?" I asked again.

"He asked if I minded working with Mae's French fiancé when they come in. Apparently he's a chef and is going to help elevate the menu. Whatever the fuck that means."

Oh, shit. "Better buckle up, buttercup. It's gonna be hard to avoid either of them."

"Tell me about it. Elevate the menu. We're a fucking Irish pub on the corner of one of the smallest towns on Keuka Lake. Is he serious?"

"Keep it down," I warned him as Beck headed over to a customer. "He's still at the bar."

Mr. O'Malley was talking to one of the customers. Beck, as usual, didn't understand the word "caution" though. It was unusual for Beck to talk poorly of his boss who he generally liked, having grown up next door to him. But everything about Mae twisted Beck into knots; not that I could judge. When Delaney and I had been on the outs, I couldn't think straight.

"I thought you talked to Mae all the time," I asked Beck when he came back. "Didn't she tell you about this?"

"She might have mentioned meeting him 'in the industry' or something. I mostly change the subject when she talks about him."

I wanted to ask if she was coming back for good or if it was a temporary thing. But changing the subject seemed prudent so I ordered a dozen wings. Just as I was finishing them up, a pair of hands covered my eyes from behind.

"Guess who?"

It was as if every shitty thing from the day melted away. Her voice soothed my soul.

"Is it a perky redheaded pharmacist?"

"Unfortunately, yes."

I grabbed her hands and spun around on the stool. "Hey. What's that supposed to mean?"

In response, Delaney kissed me and then said, "Crappy day at work."

"That must be going around."

We stared at each other. I knew where she stood with the studio. Despite the fact that everything seemed to be coming together, the idea of pulling the trigger still terrified her. Actually saying the words aloud. Telling her parents. Telling her boss. Committing to moving forward.

But I had a plan.

"I was going to wait until we were alone," I said, pulling Delaney toward me so she stood between my legs. "But I've been thinking about it all day."

"The usual?" Beck asked Delaney from behind me.

"Yes, please."

I never took my eyes from her. Hair up in a pony, her cheeks flushed red from the cold still, she looked adorable. And tired.

"Thinking about what?"

It was a huge step. Agreeing to be exclusive was one thing. Saying "I love you" another. But this... it was a risk to ask. Just thinking about that night in Manhattan and the drive back to Cedar Falls, not knowing where we stood exactly, told me all I needed to know.

I loved her. Wanted to be with her. End of story.

"I know you'll need room for storage and a workshop, in addition to the front room for classes, but there's an upstairs to the wine bar building too. If I had a room that could be turned into an office, a home base for the construction company, we could split the rent. It'll be less of a risk for you, especially as you build the business."

I managed to shock her. If it was in a good way, or a bad way, I couldn't quite tell.

"Are you serious?"

"Very. I talked to Mason about it, and he agrees I'll need a space. At first we talked about using a spare room at the inn, but that would be temporary anyway. This is a more permanent solution."

"There are two back rooms on the ground floor. You could take the bigger one. I'd use the other as a workshop and upstairs for storage. Of course"—Delaney talked quickly, her hands animated—"you would only be taking one room, so you would only pay a portion of the lease."

"No."

"No?"

"Half or nothing."

Delaney cocked her head to the side. "Now why would you pay half if you only took one room?"

"Because according to my new stepmother"—the word was getting easier to say, but still grated—"I'm a prime candidate for the size loan I need. With one job, I'd be set for six months. The profit margins with log cabin homes are insane. It will all work out. I know it. Paying half of the lease will be a drop in the bucket."

A band started playing at the other end of the bar, exactly why I'd planned to wait until later to ask her. But I hadn't been able to help it.

"You'd be seeing a lot of me."

"Another good reason to do it."

"You're serious?" she asked, smiling from ear to ear. I loved seeing Delaney so happy.

"One hundred percent."

"Then I am 100 percent in."

Grabbing her, I pulled Delaney into me, kissing her. Holding her. Forgetting that we weren't alone until Beck yelled to us, "Get a room, you two."

Delaney immediately pulled back, laughing. We spun around, and I patted the stool next to me. She sat and pulled her vodka soda toward her.

"Are Mason and Pia coming tonight?" I asked Beck, not having talked to him.

"I'm not sure."

"I haven't talked to her," Delaney said.

Pulling out my phone, I texted him. Two letters.

OM.

I wasn't at all surprised when the two of them walked in a half hour later.

"Were you guys coming anyway?" I asked as Mason greeted us. Pia had made a beeline to the bathroom, something she seemed to do a lot of these days. As a matter of fact...

"Nope. What's up?"

"We're celebrating. Round of shots," I said to Beck.

"What are we celebrating?" Mason asked.

Delaney and I exchanged a glance. We were celebrating a lot. The two of us finding each other, getting over our mutual fear of commitment. Her father making a full recovery. But this drink, this particular celebration, was for our futures as business owners.

Her eyes sparkled with excitement. "Go ahead," I told her. "Say it out loud."

Mason and Beck watched. Waited. Delaney looked for Pia, who was still gone. "I'll tell her when she gets back. So, Parker and I are co-leasing the old wine bar building on Mechanic Street. He's using it as an office for his new construction company and I'm..."

She took a deep breath. Looked at me.

I nodded.

"I'm leaving the pharmacy business behind to open an art studio."

Her eyes shone with tears. It was as scary as it was exciting. I knew the feeling all too well. But Delaney's talent and diligence would make her successful. She had everything to gain, and I couldn't wait to see what she did with the place. To share in her journey.

"Holy shit," Mason said. "Cheers to that."

"Congratulations," Beck said as he cheered and took a shot with us.

"I can't believe I just said that." Delaney did appear to be in a bit of shock.

"Said what?" Pia asked.

As she told Pia what was happening, Beck put his hands on the bar as he and Mason both looked at me.

"What?"

"Another one down," Beck said. "This is why we said to never stay the night."

"It was a good rule." I shrugged. "Looks like it's up to you and Cole now to keep the pact alive."

"That we can do. With Mae being engaged, looks like we didn't need rule number three." Beck tried to keep his voice light, but I knew better.

"At least we can count on the two of you," Mason said. "I saw you eying up that pretty blonde, but am fairly certain she isn't long-term material."

I glanced down the bar to the woman in question. She was, unsurprisingly, staring at Beck. "Being that she's barely legal?"

"Hey," Beck said. "She's twenty-two."

"You guessing or did you card her?" Mason asked.

Beck smiled. "What do you think?"

He would never change. No worries about him breaking a rule. Or Cole either, for that matter. I was almost nervous to tell him about the studio. He'd be happy for me, but there was a part of Cole that wanted all of us to really stay single with him, forever.

"I think you are a man-whore and will never change," I said, to which Mason barked out a laugh. It was true enough, though, and both of them knew it.

More importantly...

I turned to Delaney. "Hey there, cupcake. Can I get you another drink?"

She leaned toward me, whispering into my ear. "You can get me, or do to me, anything you'd like."

Just like that, the student became the teacher.

38

PARKER

"I still can't believe we have the entire inn to ourselves."

Delaney and I sat in front of the fireplace looking out onto the lake in the Eliza room, Heritage Hill's best. It would be dark soon, but the table for two with our finished takeout meal afforded a perfect view.

"Not that we're using any of it," I said, refilling our wines.

When I told Mason I wanted to do something special for Delaney to celebrate her big decision, this had been his idea. Being a Tuesday mid-winter, there were no other guests until tomorrow when this room, and the other lakeview one, would be occupied.

"It's still cool, to know we're the only ones here."

"The others are just a hallway away," I reminded her, referring to the first-floor passageway that connected the original structure from the add-on where we lived.

"True." Delaney took a sip of wine. "I just can't wait to sleep in with you tomorrow. No work. Nothing to do for the entire day. What did Jack say?"

"That I've taken more days in the past month than since I

started working for him. I figured it was as good a time as any to break it to him that I'd be taking off many more soon."

"No, you didn't?"

"I did. You inspired me."

Delaney had finally told her parents two days ago, and though they gave her a hard time, as she expected, both said that, in the end, they supported her decision. Her mother seemed more disappointed Delaney hadn't trusted her to help make the decision, thinking she would care more about the "lost" education. She admitted the risk scared her but "only because I love you and want you to be happy."

"What did he say?"

"It actually went a lot better than I expected. You know how Jack can be." In other words, the conversation might have gone in one of two ways. But instead of him telling me to fuck off, a distinct possibility, he went in the other direction.

"He said he never expected me to stay long term and was glad I decided on a niche business in construction."

"In other words, he's glad you aren't in direct competition with him."

"Exactly."

"Anything else?"

"Not really. Just that he'd help in any way he could but just asked I not leave him high and dry when I make the transition. And, of course, not to take any of the guys."

"As if you'd do either."

"Exactly."

"Wow. So we're really doing this, huh?"

I raised my glass to her and Delaney lifted her own. "We really are. Cheers, cupcake."

"Cheers," she said, reaching forward to clink my glass.

Looking down, I groaned. "Bad idea, leaning forward like that with a v-neck."

"Bad idea? Or good idea?"

So she wanted to get spicy, huh? "You're right." I put down my glass, stood up and pulled Delaney out of her seat. "A good idea. A very, very good idea."

Before she could prepare for what I was about to do, I lifted the henley shirt up and over her head. Instead of stopping there to enjoy the fruits of my labor, I unzipped her jeans and got rid of those just as quickly.

Before long, we were divested of our clothing and Delaney found herself positioned perfectly in the middle of the bed. I wanted to touch every inch of her. I wanted to make her wild with my tongue, showing her why I hadn't ordered dessert with the meal.

But more than anything, I wanted to make love to her.

Positioning myself between her legs, after a quick check to ensure she was wet with such little foreplay—she was—I didn't screw around. Guiding myself into her, we became one. Despite the frantic pace of our disrobing, evidenced by clothes strewn around the bed, this was anything but frantic.

"I am so in love with you, Delaney Montana Thorton."

"Mmmm, thought maybe you forgot about that," she said, pulling me all the way down, on top of her.

"Never. I love it. Someday we're going there to make love in a log cabin in the mountains." Our pace was slow, deliberate. Delaney held me close to her, as if I wanted to go anywhere. The feel of her breasts against my chest, of being inside her... never. I wasn't going anywhere, ever.

Reaching down between us, I circled my thumb against her clit, looking forward to seeing her face when Delaney came for me.

"We're going to make love in a balcony room with a view of the Mediterranean in Italy," I said, increasing the pace. "And everywhere and anywhere else you want to go."

"Promise?"

"I promise, cupcake. Now why don't you show me how that pretty face of yours lights up as you come all over me. My fingers..."

"Parker."

"My dick."

"Parker."

"Come on, that's it." Her hips circled below me, the slow pace giving way to something more urgent.

When Delaney began to cry out, I removed my hand and thrust into her. Holding myself there, I was completely buried in her. I could feel Delaney's orgasm as my own had me driving even deeper. She clung to me as I cried out, every muscle in my body tensing.

Neither of us let go, for a long time.

When we finally did manage to move and find ourselves in the massive whirlpool tub, I vowed to install one in our own master bedroom.

"I want one of these in our log cabin," I said, my hand running over Delaney's outer thigh as she lay between my legs. Under the premise of "cleaning" her with the small bar of soap in my hand, I explored every inch of her body.

"A log cabin, huh?"

"That alright with you?"

Delaney moved to the side, looking up at me. "More than alright. Are you being serious though?"

"Very. Maybe lakeside?"

She laughed. "A log cabin on the lake. That sounds... expensive."

"The land, maybe. But if I can build the house at cost, not as much. Besides, we'll both have successful businesses by then."

"You think so?"

"I know so."

"You're being serious."

"Very serious," I assured her. "What else do you want? Hot tub on the deck, obviously."

"Obviously." Delaney sighed and moved back against my chest.

I would have to talk to Pia about how to propose. It had to be special, like the woman nestled between my legs. But I would propose and make Delaney my wife. Yesterday, she told me that she wanted to spend the rest of her life with me after I'd asked her if she could see herself getting married, and that had sealed the deal.

"We should probably talk about living arrangements in the meantime."

"I actually don't mind how it is now. Unless that's a pain for you, being part time at the inn and part time at my place?"

"It's fine. If that works for you."

"For now it does," I said. "I can keep helping Mason renovate the inn while putting all of the pieces of the new business in place. I think by the end of spring, we'll have everything finished."

"Speaking of timelines..."

We talked about our new businesses, of our future. We talked until both Delaney and I were wrinkled, a signal for us to finally get out.

We were dressed in thick white robes, and I pulled her toward me, kissing the woman that would, someday, become my wife.

"To think all of this happened," she said, "because you broke one of the rules."

"Never stay the night." I smiled. "I'm glad I broke it. Glad I won't be collecting that money."

"Who do you think will?"

"Between Beck and Cole? That's anyone's guess. All that matters is, not me."

"I'm glad you broke it too. Now let's go get some sleep."

Following her into the bedroom, I didn't correct her. If Delaney thought we'd get sleep tonight, with neither of us working in the morning, she hadn't been paying attention.

Thankfully, I was a patient teacher.

EPILOGUE
DELANEY

"Talk about déjà vu," I said, glancing around the log cabin where it had all started. Like that first time, it was snowing outside, but this time, just lightly. Thankfully not enough to cancel the trip, especially for Cole, who'd come in for the weekend. And it was his colleague, after all, who'd loaned us the place.

"With one major difference." Pia lifted up her iced tea.

Mason made a face that said he was thankful it was Pia, and not him, who couldn't drink.

"The sacrifices you make," Beck called from the great room. He was still "warming up" by the fire despite the fact that we got here a half hour ago.

"That's enough from the peanut gallery," Pia said. "Where did Cole disappear to?"

"He's checking on the hot tub." Parker smiled at me. Was he remembering our first time in that tub? Most likely. I definitely was.

"When the two of you are finished eye fucking each other, can we talk about dinner?"

"I said," Parker countered, "either is fine with me."

More accustomed now to Mason's blunt nature, I didn't take offense. "Same," I said. "Let the preggo girl decide."

We had all been shocked when Pia and Mason told us. Although they'd been planning for a small wedding at the inn, the surprise news had them moving up the date from October to June. Apparently, although they hadn't been trying for a baby already, they hadn't been actively trying to avoid getting pregnant. And, voila.

If we thought Mason was protective before, he was downright vigilante now. Just the other day he'd found her using Windex and hired the inn's cleaning lady to start doing the house portion of Heritage Hill too, despite the fact that Pia insisted using it was safe for the baby.

"Pizza," Pia declared. "And breadsticks. With marinara sauce."

"Do they have breadsticks?" I asked, pulling the takeout menu toward me.

"Doesn't matter. Mason will find them either way," Parker teased. "He'll drive back to Cedar Falls if necessary."

It had become a running joke, Mason's... vigilance with Pia.

"Fuck you," Mason said.

"Love you too," Parker responded.

A typical exchange on a typical Friday night, except we were in a multi-million-dollar ski chalet, celebrating. "Oh, shit," I said, thinking of that. "I was supposed to bring champagne. It's on my kitchen counter."

"Luckily for you, I remembered how forgetful you are and re-checked the kitchen, and bedroom, before we left. I've got it. And your toiletry bag too, which was sitting on your sink."

Jumping off my stool, I went over to him, kissing Parker on the cheek for his thoughtfulness. At least, I tried to kiss him on the cheek but he turned his head. Not wanting to full-on make out in front of our friends, I broke it off with a whisper of, "There'll be more where that came from later."

"Yeah, there will," he said back, earning an eye roll from Mason. "Why wait," Parker said as Cole came back inside.

"It's cold as balls out there," he said. "But the hot tub is on."

"Another thing I can't do," Pia said, pretending to be sad. Or maybe she was actually sad, though I doubted it. She was so thrilled with the baby that all of us had been on pins and needles until she hit three months.

"I can think of something we can do instead." Mason to the rescue.

"And you bust my ass." Parker pulled me into his side. Apparently I wasn't going back to my stool.

"You're all ridiculous." Cole went to a cabinet and began pulling out champagne glasses. "No time like the present," he said, putting them in a row before taking off his glasses and cleaning them on his sweater.

"Can we order food first?" Mason asked.

Everyone ignored him. I managed to disengage myself from Parker and headed to the fridge. "Beck," I called as Cole popped the bottle and poured each of us a glass. Except poor Pia, who got Sprite instead.

"Come on, Beck," Pia called. Once everyone had a glass, she did the toast.

"To the last day of work for you both," she said to Parker and me. Neither Parker nor I had planned to quit our jobs before spring, but as we both became busier and busier with the new businesses, it was apparent something had to give. We'd each gotten a loan which would carry us into the summer for income, and so we coordinated it, yesterday being both of our last days on the job.

A bittersweet ending to my short career as a pharmacist. On one hand, I was so excited to begin a new chapter. On the other, it was still scary as hell, a little less so because I had someone on the journey with me.

"To endings and new beginnings," he continued. "Bound by life's ride, here's to the journey."

"Here's to the journey," we all repeated, drinking. Except, while I finished my champagne, Parker got off his stool. It took me a second to figure out why.

He was down on one knee next to me.

"Delaney Thorton," he said. I looked around at each of the faces, and none of them seemed surprised. They'd all known it was coming.

I glanced back at Parker, who had an open ring box lifted up to me. Inside, an absolutely beautiful emerald-cut engagement ring.

"I asked Pia how to do this to make it special. We thought of all different ways, and clever scenarios. But in the end, what really matters are the people. Everyone in this room loves us both and wants to see us happy, so it made sense to ask you with our second family surrounding us... will you do me the honor of becoming my wife?"

By the time he'd finished, tears streamed down my cheeks. "This weekend," I managed, thinking about how it had all come together.

"We're celebrating our engagement," he said. "If you say yes."

I'd forgotten to say yes. My mind was a jumbled mess of happiness. "Of course. Yes, yes, yes," I said as Parker slipped the ring on my finger and everyone cheered and clapped around us.

"We're getting married," I whispered to him as Parker stood and hugged me.

"Yes, we are, cupcake. Thank you for making me the happiest man in the world."

"Ditto," I said, wishing I could have been more eloquent, like him. But it didn't matter. What mattered was the smiling faces all around us, even the two guys who still didn't believe in love. Hopefully, like Mason and Parker had, someone would come along to change their minds too.

* * *

MORE FROM CISSY MECCA

Another book from Cissy Mecca, *Fallen Hearts*, is available to order now here:

https://mybook.to/FallenHeartsBackAd

ABOUT THE AUTHOR

Cissy Mecca is the author of the American small-town romance series such as *The Bachelor Pact* and *The Boys of Bridgewater*. She also writes spicy romantasy under the pen name C. L. Mecca. She lives in Northeast Pennsylvania with her family.

Sign up to Cissy Mecca's mailing list for news, competitions and updates on future books.

Follow Cissy on social media here:

facebook.com/MeccaRomance
instagram.com/meccaromance
tiktok.com/@clmeccaauthor

ALSO BY CISSY MECCA

Cedar Falls Series

Fallen Hearts

Desired Hearts

Cissy Mecca writing as C. L. Mecca

Whisper of War and Storms

Tide of Waves and Secrets

EVER AFTER

xoxo

JOIN BOLDWOOD'S
**ROMANCE
COMMUNITY**
FOR SWEET AND
SPICY BOOK RECS
WITH ALL YOUR
FAVOURITE
TROPES!

SIGN UP TO OUR
NEWSLETTER

HTTPS://BIT.LY/BOLDWOODEVERAFTER

Boldwood

Boldwood Books is an award-winning fiction publishing company seeking out the best stories from around the world.

Find out more at www.boldwoodbooks.com

Join our reader community for brilliant books, competitions and offers!

Follow us
@BoldwoodBooks
@TheBoldBookClub

Sign up to our weekly deals newsletter

https://bit.ly/BoldwoodBNewsletter